# THE LAST SOLDIER

Rich Hawkins lives in Salisbury, England, with his wife and daughter. He has several short stories published in various anthologies. 'The Last Soldier' is the final book in his 'Plague' Trilogy. The Last Plague was nominated for a British Fantasy Award in 2015.

# THE LAST SOLDIER

RICH HAWKINS

Copyright © 2015 Rich Hawkins

This Edition Published 2016 by Crowded Quarantine Publications
The moral right of the author has been asserted

All characters in this publication are fictitious and any resemblance to real persons, living or dead, is purely coincidental.

All rights reserved.
No part of this publication may be reproduced, stored in a retrieval system, or transmitted, in any form or by any means without the prior permission in writing of the publisher, nor be otherwise circulated in any form of binding or cover other than that in which it is published and without a similar condition including this condition being imposed on the subsequent purchase.

A CIP catalogue record for this book is available from the British Library

ISBN: 978-0-9932070-0-6

Crowded Quarantine Publications
34 Cheviot Road
Wolverhampton
West Midlands
WV2 2HD

*For Sara, Willow, and Molly.*

# PART ONE

# THE PLAGUE ISLES

# THE LAST SOLDIER

# PROLOGUE

The fleet of refugee boats left the beach behind and speared through the water towards the grey hulks of the waiting battleships. Florence looked back for Frank and Ralph, but there were only the swarms of infected on the beach, mired and thrashing among the remains of dead refugees. And when the immense guns of the Royal Navy opened fire she covered her ears and screamed, because she knew her dear Frank was gone.

\*

A refugee camp on the shore of a Norwegian fjord. Canvas tents and makeshift shelters made of wood and sheets of metal. Widows and orphans, grief and desperation. Silent men smoked their last cigarettes, and rows of people waited in line for bowls of soup served by pale young men with shaved heads.

Beyond the shore, the HMS *Bulwark* dwelled on the dark water. The snow-capped mountains high above the camp were grand and beautiful and reduced Florence to silent awe. The air was cold and she pulled her coat and the blanket tighter around her shoulders.

Joel and Anya comforted her when she cried, and she cried many times during those early days. They drank soup from their bowls, but were still hungry. Always hungry. Second helpings were forbidden and no amount of pleading swayed the solemn-faced soldiers.

They were traumatised, displaced people sheltering from the terror of a new world. The horror of the plague in their memories. Survivors' guilt gnawed at their hearts. Minds numbed and broken. Withered faces. Exhaustion and despair. Some of them gathered on the shore to grieve together, while others prayed and sang hymns. Others screamed at the sky and said the names of loved ones left behind.

\*

Latrines were dug out of the ground. The pages of books were ripped out to use as toilet paper. The smell of piss soaked into the ground. It rained most days and when it didn't rain it snowed, and no one ever smiled because it would be obscene and there was already enough misery to be shared amongst the broken people.

The medical station was always busy. Florence thought often of her parents and Frank. She tried to cry no more because she didn't want Joel and Anya to see, but even when she hid her face with her hands they knew and they went to her, and Anya held her and whispered folk songs from Poland.

And in the sky, the Plague Gods wailed mournfully.

\*

Joel and Anya were married by an army captain in a simple ceremony just after the first Christmas at the camp, gathered on the shore as snow fell on the dark water in the silvery gleam of the moon. Joel had already thrown his crucifix necklace away and told Florence to never believe the lies of pious men.

\*

The weather grew colder. The rations were reduced to measly handfuls. One cup of water a day. Sickness in the camp. Nightmares every night. The winter killed many, and by the end of it the population of the camp had dwindled to a third of its original number. People died in their tents while others simply followed the winding trails into the mountains and never returned.

Joel found Anya dead by the shore one night. The place where they'd been married. He held her body and cried, cursed God and spat when he said His name. Florence stood away from them and felt such despair that she fell to her knees, put her hands to her face and started sobbing.

The HMS *Bulwark* left the fjord and took the soldiers away.

A few days later, after he'd buried his wife, Joel opened his wrists with a straight razor at the water's edge. Florence dragged his body to Anya's grave and it took her all of a day and most of a night to dig a hole for him. And when she was finished she slumped on the ground and passed out, and only woke when someone screamed from the far end of the camp.

The screams never lasted long.

She mourned Joel and Anya, as she did the others. Her parents. Frank, Ralph and Magnus. She mourned for the infected too. And afterwards she only left her tent to scavenge supplies from the scraps the soldiers had left behind.

At least now she had extra blankets.

# CHAPTER ONE

Florence sat in the back of the rowboat and trailed her hand in the cold, dark water. She wondered of the beasts lurking below the calm surface of the sea: squid and whales, weird fish with bulging eyes and gaping mouths; half-blind things and pale arachnids hunting in deep fathoms and oblivion black. Abyssal trenches no man had ever seen.

The mist was all about them, obscuring the shore they approached. Florence lifted her hand from the water and dried it on her ill-fitting coat then pulled her woollen hat down over the tops of her ears. She hugged her rucksack tight to her body, and when the rowboat swayed she tried to dispel the image of something with a giant mouth hurtling upwards towards the underside of the boat.

Morse sat at the bow, facing the shore, the rifle held across his body. He turned back to Florence and nodded. She returned the gesture because that was all she could think to do. She noticed the trembling of her legs beneath her. The fluttering in her heart only faded when she took shallow gulps of air.

Between them, Henrik worked the oars, boots braced against the uprights, his breath like mist in the cold air and his forehead damp with sweat. He said nothing, and the only sounds were of the oars slicing the water and scraping against the rowlocks on either side.

The shore appeared out of the mist. A grey beach and spikes of seagrass beyond. Henrik stopped rowing and turned to Morse. "I go no further."

Morse hefted his pack and hooked it over one shoulder. Florence glanced down at the water and shivered. Morse caught her looking.

"It's the shallows, Florence. Henrik wouldn't drop us too far off shore. He's not a complete arsehole, you know."

The Norwegian snorted. "Lucky I come this far, Morse. I get nothing for this but wet fucking feet and sore arms. English bastard."

There was a low splash as Morse jumped into the water. His face tightened at the cold as he looked at Florence. "I'll carry you. Hurry up."

"I'm not scared of the water." She stood and tottered, raising her arms for balance. Henrik offered no assistance and just watched without expression. Morse lifted her from the boat, and when he lowered her into the water it reached her knees. Her heartbeat spiked at the shocking cold. Water sprayed on her face;

she spat and wiped her mouth. All she wanted was to get out of the water, even if the monsters waited for them on the shore.

Morse nodded at Henrik. "Tell your captain we're even now. And give him my regards."

Henrik scratched his grey beard then took the oar handles in his hands. "I will."

"Thank you, Henrik. Now row back to your ship before the infected bite your stupid fucking arse."

Henrik began rowing away, back towards the trawler waiting in the mist. Within seconds he had disappeared.

Morse took hold of Florence's arm and pulled her through the shallows and onto the beach. When she stumbled and fell, Morse helped her back up and brushed sand from her clothes.

"Welcome to Scotland," he said.

# CHAPTER TWO

They kept low to the ground as they moved from the damp beach to a crumbling stone wall beyond the banks of seagrass. Thick mist surrounded them. They crouched. Florence gasped for breath, shaking inside her clothes. Morse slung the strap of the rifle around his neck and watched the mist move. Then he pulled the compass and map from one pocket of his tactical vest.

"Where are we?" Florence said, keeping close to the wall. She glanced about, fretting with the straps of her rucksack. Her feet were soaking wet.

Morse studied the map. "I think we're a mile or two south of Eyemouth. If we were dropped in the right place, of course."

A slow drizzle began to fall, so Florence pulled her hood up and turned her face from the sky. "Is that good?"

"It's neither good nor bad. This was as far as the ship could take us from Norway. We were lucky they took us this far. It's up to you now, Florence."

"I knew you were going to say that."

"This was your idea."
"I know."
"You ready for this?"
"I don't know."
"Okay. Let's go."

\*

They walked through a weed-ridden car park where someone had arranged the bones of a small animal on the cracked tarmac, and then onto a road flanked by scrubland and wire fences, some of which had collapsed during the two years since the outbreak. Morse scanned the toiling mist with his rifle and moved alongside Florence so that she was within an arm's reach. He glanced at the girl and had a sudden feeling he was a fool for following her back to Britain. But there was nothing else to be done. Even the last outpost at Esjberg was under constant attack. He saw a future where humans were reduced to the remnants of feral tribes, hiding from the infected in dark holes and isolated hovels, the population past the point of no return for the species. And how many people were left alive? Probably not enough to start again. Perhaps it was time to accept the inevitable: the extinction of humans from the world.

Florence stared at the sky as she walked. Morse wondered what she saw. She was not an ordinary girl. She had a gift.

"Is this the right way?" Morse asked.

"Don't you trust me?"

He wiped his mouth. "I'm not sure I trust the thing inside your head."

She turned and her large eyes regarded him from within rings of bruised skin. She looked tired and pitiable, wrapped up and shuddering underneath her clothes.

"Sorry," Morse said. "I shouldn't have said that."

She faced down the road. "It's okay. I don't trust it either."

\*

They halted at a crossroads and Morse checked his watch. "We've got a few hours before it gets dark. We'll have to find somewhere to stay for the night."

Something shrieked out in the mist. They froze. There were other sounds – mewling, wet clicking, and crying – as though a herd of animals were bogged down in treacherous marshland and couldn't escape. Morse raised the rifle. Florence stood close to him and trembled.

\*

The sleet fell faster and thicker as they walked, and Morse had to shield his eyes with one hand while he tried to keep watch over the road and the surrounding fields. The spiked trees were knotted black growths sprouting from the soil.

Florence walked with her head bowed and arms folded. Such a slight form inside her oversized coat. Twin plumes of misted breath drifted from her nose. She muttered something Morse couldn't quite hear.

There were more sounds in the mist. The hair stood up on the back of Morse's neck and his guts churned and reared. He looked to his right and thought he saw movement far across the field, but it was only there for a second, and he didn't look for long because the sleet on his shoulders was pushing him down, wearing him down. The wind pulled at his body and tested his strength. He felt tired, old and worn out. Perhaps he had already lived too long in a world where untold numbers were dead. A man in his previous line of work was lucky to reach fifty, and he was a few years beyond that and still taking breath.

He started at a sound that might have been a crow cawing from a treetop. He raised the rifle and licked water from his lips. Breathed in deep and held it until his lungs tightened. The mist muffled sounds then amplified them when it cleared for a moment to reveal old farmland being slowly retaken by nature. Fields changing to meadows of sickly-looking vegetation. Everything gone-to-seed, desolate and withered in the winter. There were no animals to be seen, and he wondered if the infected had wiped out the wildlife once the human survivors had dwindled.

Morse stopped. It was difficult to see beyond ten yards. The wet road was cracked and swollen where tree roots had spread under the tarmac. Weeds were sprouting through the fractures.

"We should find somewhere to shelter."

Florence halted beside him. "How far have we walked?"

"Maybe a mile or two."

"Is that all?"

"Afraid so."

"Feels like more."

"Always does."

\*

The low, blunt shape of a car appeared out of the mist, skewed across the road and blocking their path. Morse kept Florence behind him as he moved towards the vehicle with the rifle pressed to his shoulder. Then he halted and let out a slow breath that blended with the mist. When he noticed it was a Vauxhall Vectra, he snorted as he recalled he used to own one in the long ago.

Flat tyres cracked and worn, sagging and airless. Rusted metal and flaking paint. There was a dirty handprint smeared across one of the windows. The bonnet was open and leaves and bits of straw and grass covered the exposed parts of the engine. Faint smell of oil when he lowered his head closer to the bonnet. He looked through a window and lowered the rifle.

"Is it okay?" Florence said from back down the road. She held her gloved hands together and glanced around.

Morse signalled her over.

She came over and stood beside him, scrutinizing the jumble of browned human bones in the front passenger footwell. Her eyes lingered on a stained jawbone.

"I wonder who it was," she said.

"It doesn't matter. None of it matters. You know that, Florence."

\*

Half a mile further on, Florence stopped in the road and turned her head to the right like she was tracking something unseen through the mist. She stared for a long while, and Morse followed her gaze, but saw nothing and the mist remained undisturbed.

As they walked onwards, Morse scanned the area behind them then faced down the road again and made sure Florence didn't get too far ahead.

\*

They found a dead man by the side of the road. The right side of his body was covered in blackened cysts and drooping cilia, and the skin of his right arm was peeled back to reveal a fleshy proboscis all red and slack. Its tip was needle-like. Flaps of putrefying skin covered bulging tumours. Busy teeth had been at his face and his eyes were gone. A pale, withered thing, nothing more than carrion for the scavengers, stinking of sickly sweet rot.

Morse frowned. "Christ."

Florence stepped towards the body, but Morse laid a hand on her shoulder and held her back. "Leave it alone."

The girl stared at the man. "Who was he?"

"It doesn't matter now."

"It matters to me."

Morse withdrew his hand. "Come on. Let's find somewhere to wait out the weather."

"I'm sorry," Florence said as they stepped away. And it was only when they walked down the road and she looked back that Morse realised she was talking to the dead man.

# CHAPTER THREE

The sleet turned to rain and they crouched against a tree trunk, huddled together and keeping watch like lost soldiers of a defeated army. They stayed there for a while. The branches were bare and offered little shelter from the downpour. Florence recited a nursery rhyme as she looked out at the land. She was very pale and her bloodshot eyes never stayed on one place for long.

Morse leant on his rifle, blowing into his hands. His boots sunk into the dirt beneath the wet layer of leaves, bark scrapings and pine needles. Florence startled him when she pointed suddenly in the direction she'd been looking.

"There's a house over there."

Morse wiped his eyes. "Where?"

"I just saw it. Only a glimpse, but I definitely saw it."

Morse stared out to where she pointed, but it was impossible to see through the mist and rain that conspired against them. "How far away?"

"Not far, I think."

"You're sure?"

She regarded him with the tired eyes of someone much older. "Would you rather stay here?"

\*

Morse followed her into the mist. Further on the house appeared out of the murk, and Florence halted and turned back to him. Inside her hood, she smiled sadly and her face was damp with rain. A haunted girl who communed with monsters and pestilent minds.

\*

They approached the cottage from the north side and kept low to the ground as they stumbled over puddles and muddy divots. Florence tripped on a molehill but Morse steadied her and stopped her from falling. They halted within thirty yards of the cottage, peering over the rim of a ditch beginning to flood with rainwater. The downpour gave no respite. Morse looked to the sky and saw no end to the grey clouds. What he would give to see the sun again.

"You think someone's in there?" Florence sniffed and wiped her nose, bunching her shoulders against the rain.

Morse pulled out his binoculars. Nothing moved around the house. He watched the windows, but it was too dark inside the house to notice anyone standing beyond the glass.

"Maybe. Hard to tell."

"Bad people?"

"What?"

"Bandits or marauders. Murderers. Cannibals."

"Cannibals?"

"You told me about what happened in that refugee shelter in Sweden. Remember?"

"That was just a rumour."

"People who eat people."

Morse exhaled through his nose. "That's right."

"Do you think the only survivors left in Britain are bad people?"

"I think people do what they have to do to survive."

"Have you ever eaten someone?"

"Yes."

"Really?"

"No."

"Oh." She hesitated. "Would you, if you had to?"

"I don't know. Probably not."

"Okay."

The wind whistled along the ditch and faded into a mournful sigh. Morse lowered the binoculars. "Looks empty. Follow me and stay close."

They stood with their backs flat against the side of the house. Florence was breathing hard as she squeezed her hands into fists and held them to her chest. Morse checked the AK-47 and listened to the rain pattering upon dead leaves and mud. The front garden was overgrown and dripping, frothing with dense foliage and limp weeds. He pulled Florence along as he edged to the front corner of the cottage and then gestured for her to stay where he left her. Then he stepped around the corner with the rifle raised, watching the windows. He placed his feet carefully, alert for traps and snares. The front door was shut. He cast a glance at the garden to make sure nothing was waiting in ambush then moved to the door and turned the handle and it opened first time. A dull click as he twisted. He used his free hand to push the door open, and he entered the house, bracing himself for a bullet or blade. The familiar pressure tightened his chest and squeezed his stomach. He moved in silence and found himself in a large kitchen where everything was covered in dust. Bare plaster had crumbled from the walls to scatter on the floor and along the skirting boards.

A wheatsheaf nailed to a wooden upright. A Bonsai tree dried to dusty sticks. Upon the far wall, a watercolour seascape. A rotting wooden crucifix on the wall above the AGA stove. Pots and pans in mouldering piles on the floor. The scratching of sightless things in the walls.

On the dining table, beside a pile of faded newspapers, a human skull grinned on a plate, furred by dust, a memento of an atrocity in the dark places. Morse stared at its empty sockets and the leathery patches of skin still clinging to its jaw and scalp.

"A warm welcome," he whispered, and shook his head.

He removed the skull before he summoned Florence inside.

# CHAPTER FOUR

Morse drew his pistol from the chest holster. The dull light through the windows. The rain on the roof. Smell of mothballs and wood varnish. Old furniture riddled with stains. Something moved in the walls and shadowed his path along a corridor. He remembered catching and eating a rat with some other survivors in the ruins of a refugee camp. A brief image of their faces. He couldn't even recall their names, but it didn't matter, because they were dead and gone, beyond all the pain and suffering in the world.

The downstairs rooms were deserted. The kitchen, the living room, and a small bathroom at the back of the house. Family photos. He expected to find bones, but there were none. When he checked the cupboard under the stairs, the gleaming eyes of rodents stared back at him from the darkness between stacks of boxes. He shut the door quickly and stepped away.

*

Morse left Florence in the kitchen while he went upstairs into rooms of shadows and dust. Peeling wallpaper spotted with black mould beneath cobwebs and desiccated insects out of reach in high corners. There was nothing useful in the deserted rooms so he returned downstairs and found Florence staring at the plate he had found the human skull upon.

"You okay?" he said.

She looked up and nodded, then turned away.

"You sure?"

"Tired."

"Same here."

"But that's because you're old, Morse."

"Cheeky sod. I'm not pushing up daisies yet."

"What does that mean?"

"It's an old saying."

"I don't understand."

"Doesn't matter."

\*

They secured the doors and stuffed old rags into the holes in the windows. Florence winced at the sound of distant thunder. The deluge against the outside of the cottage was so loud that she covered her ears. Morse stood by the living room window and looked outside and the world was lost to the rain.

Thunder crackled again. Closer this time. When he turned around, Florence had slumped on the tattered sofa staring at one of the family photos on the wall.

"I don't like the thunder," she said.

Morse unshouldered his rucksack. "Are you hungry?"

She shook her head.

"You have to eat something, to keep your energy up. Did you have any breakfast on the ship?"

"Just some water and a stale biscuit."

"You'll get weak."

"I'm already weak."

"You know what I mean."

"I know."

"Okay."

"Okay."

He sighed. "Looks like we'll be staying here a little while. Best to get some chow and rest up while we can."

"What if the rain doesn't stop? Will we stay here for the night?"

Morse chewed his lip. "Maybe. Let's just see what happens. Would you mind doing that?"

"I don't know." She appraised the room around her. "It's okay now, but it might be different when it's dark."

He pulled a chocolate bar from his pack and threw it to her. She caught it in two hands. "Eat some food. Rest. I'll keep watch."

She tore the wrapping from the chocolate bar, took a bite and chewed, staring at the floor. She devoured the chocolate in seconds then folded the wrapper and tucked it down the back of the sofa.

Morse watched the rain.

"Can I ask you something, Morse?"

"Of course. Always."

"Do you think this house is haunted?"

He nearly smiled, but thought better of it. "I wouldn't worry. The whole world is full of ghosts."

# CHAPTER FIVE

Florence knew she was dreaming when the front door opened and the family that used to live in the house walked in. The house smelled clean and there were no spots of black mould on the walls. This was a time before the outbreak, and she was reduced to silence as she sat in the living room, on the sofa that was no longer tattered and faded.

She watched them with tears in her eyes. A mum and dad, a young boy, and a small dog that ran to her and licked her hands. She stroked the dog's head and watched the family unpack their shopping. Bags of frozen food. Ice cream, pizza, chips. Donuts and crisps. Cheese and butter. Fresh vegetables and fizzy drinks.

The dog nuzzled her fingers with a wet nose.

Then she was sitting at the dining table with the family while the dog loitered around them waiting for scraps. They talked about films, music, football, books. Homework. The parents spoke to the boy about his last school report. She remembered her school and all her friends and the teachers. She supposed they were dead, and the flashbulb memory of their faces formed such a feeling of loss inside her she could only bow her head and close her eyes.

The family ignored her when she began crying, so she slammed her hands on the table and kept banging until she could do it no more and her mouth opened into a scream while the family ate their dinner and discussed the old world she remembered and mourned in her dreams.

\*

Morse woke Florence and held her as she cried.

"It's okay," he whispered. "It's okay. You fell asleep, that's all. It's just a dream."

She pressed her face against his shoulder and spoke through her tears. "I hate dreaming."

"I know."

"That dead man we found by the roadside. He lived here with his family. I recognised him in one of the photos on the walls."

"It's okay."

"They were happy, I think."

"I know."

She wiped her eyes and sniffled. "I wonder what happened to their dog."

The rain stopped late in the day and by then it was too soon before dusk to leave the house. The light faded from the sky until it was full dark. The mist cleared soon afterwards.

Near midnight Morse watched over Florence as she slept in her sleeping bag, swaddled in the blankets he'd found upstairs. He sat on an uncomfortable wooden stool by the window; he knew that if he sat in the armchair next to the sofa he'd get too comfortable and fall asleep. The blanket over his shoulders did little to stop the cold. His rifle stood against the wall near to his right hand.

There was nothing beyond the window but the starless black. He hadn't lit a candle because he could see fine in the dark, a shadow amongst the other shadows. And he listened to the house in the night, its gentle sighs and muffled creaks, the whispers in pipes in the walls. He looked back at Florence and wondered what dwelled in her dreams. He couldn't imagine the things inside her head. She had told him of voices in her dreams which begged her for help; but she could never help them because they were beyond her and lost in the dark.

There was a slight frown on her face. The slow rise and fall of her chest. Morse considered the possibility that he was being misled. Was she still human? Was she a monster wearing the skin of a girl? But it mattered little, because whatever she was, he had promised to protect her, and he would keep that oath until he was dead.

He took the knife from his belt and picked dirt from under his fingernails. Then he ran the tip of the blade along the scars on his wrists and listened to the silence in the night around the house.

\*

Morse woke with a gasp in the first shades of daylight. He raised his face from his chest and blinked, picking crust from the corners of his eyes. The knife was still in his hand, and after he returned it to the sheath he stood and turned to check on Florence, but she was already standing behind him.

"Morning," she said.

Morse frowned. "Morning. You startled me."

"Sorry."

"How long have you been awake?"

"Not long. Are we leaving soon? I don't like it here. The house keeps talking to me."

\*

After a breakfast of old MREs and some water, they left the house with Florence leading the way. Morse watched her. A raggedy girl wrapped up in her coat and thick scarf, traipsing across the mud and leaf mulch.

They walked for over an hour, bypassing the dark apparitions of villages and towns left deserted in the aftermath of the plague. A blackened church spire in a ruined hamlet. An abandoned roadworks, rusted tools in the roadside grass. A corpse without shoes. Fallen and splintered trees beyond an area charred and ashen from an old wildfire. Florence stared at a pit of burnt human remains in a dismal field.

Morse grimaced at his aching legs and pined for the days when he was young and his heart was strong. A lot had happened since then and he'd seen things that would never leave him, and that was even before the outbreak. He thought of old friends and comrades, good mates, all of them long gone.

Florence stopped in the road to look at the sky. The pale clouds with smudges of grey and ash. Morse stood beside her and noticed two of her fingers rubbing together by her side. A shadow passed over her face and the pupils in her eyes diminished to pin pricks.

"I can feel them inside my head," she said. "It's like a worm that never stops burrowing through my brain."

"I've got some paracetamol, if you think it'll help."

"Pills don't work much."

"Do you need to stop for a while?"

"No." A pause. Then: "We could be losing our minds. We could be mad. Both of us."

"My ex-wife thought I was mad."

"Which one?"

"The first. She said I was unhinged."

"Would we even realise? In this world?"

"Probably not."

"Does that worry you?"

"I worry about you, Florence."

She lowered her face and looked at him. Her cheeks were reddish and puffy from the cold. "You don't have to worry. What will happen, will happen. There's nothing to be done about it."

Morse wiped his mouth. "We'll do what we can."

"Even that might not be enough."

# CHAPTER SIX

The flat countryside in shades of corrosion. The caterwaul of the wind past farmhouses and empty cow sheds. Deer fed on the sparse grass in desolate fields and glanced about themselves for predators. They watched Morse and Florence travel the road.

More bones in the dirt and on the flaking tarmac. Tufts of fur on barbed wire. A child's toy. The guts of electrical appliances in rotting sacks. They passed a tree where dripping rags hung from its low branches like pagan decorations. Further on a tractor had been overturned in a ditch and was slowly being smothered by creeping brambles and vines. Morse told Florence to avoid the poison hemlock growing at the roadsides.

They weaved through places in the road where car accidents were frozen in time and glass granules crackled under their boots. The insides of some cars were stained with old blood. Florence peered through a window then immediately stepped away and didn't tell Morse what she'd seen.

"Keep moving," he said. "No point in lingering here." He picked up a crumpled hubcap, threw it into the adjacent field and watched it spin in the air until it flopped in the dirt. Everything faded and solemn below the gunmetal sky.

"At least it's not raining," he said.

*

They stopped to rest in the late morning and shared a muesli bar. Morse kept watch while he chewed.

"Tastes like sawdust," Florence said, picking something from her tongue and flicking it away.

"I think it's ninety percent sawdust and the rest of it is rabbit droppings." Morse tucked the wrapper into one pocket. "But don't knock it too much; it's better than some of the stuff I've eaten."

"Did you ever eat rabbit droppings?" Florence said. "Grilled."

She looked at him. Her brow creased. "Really?"

"Nah."

"I knew it."

"They were scrambled actually."

"What about cow dung?"

"Of course. Raw. Tasty."

"You're lying."

"Would I lie to you?"

"Yes."

"That's not a very nice thing to say."

"Shut up, Morse."

"Yes, M'lady."

When she let out a small laugh, Morse's heart swelled and he fought a smile at the edges of his mouth. It was good to hear. He looked up the road in the direction they were heading. "Ready to go?"

She was already on her feet. She nodded. Morse grabbed his rifle and they carried on.

\*

Morse thought he heard distant calls on the wind and wasn't sure who or what they were from, or if they were merely auditory hallucinations. Figments. He scanned the fields, kept a watch. Always watching.

To the east, far from the roadside, blackened beams jutted from the half-collapsed wreck of a house. His gaze lingered until the ruins passed out of view behind a dull thicket. He could smell ash and rotting vegetation. Animal scents. Damp matted grass. His boots crunched on wet gravel.

The road widened until it became a dual carriageway flanked by ground that rose into steep banks of earth. There were no vehicles left behind, just tyre marks on the tarmac and ghost-shapes of leaked oil. Down the middle of the carriageway was a median strip of grass and steel ropes mounted on posts. Morse watched their flanks, wary and nervous. Ahead of them, a bridge ran across the carriageway, and when they reached it they stopped beneath for a moment and drank some water. Florence stared past Morse. She scratched the skin under her right eye.

"There's something down the road," she said.

Morse took the binoculars and looked. There was a flicker of movement past a pile up of several cars that stretched across their side of the carriageway. It was hard to make out anything. A moving shadow, a smoke-shape.

Morse lowered the binoculars.

"What is it?" Florence said. "Infected?"

"I don't know. Stay behind me." He put the binoculars away then raised the rifle to his chest. "Let's go."

\*

When they rounded the pile up, they came across a pack of feral dogs tearing at a deer carcass. They were mostly mongrels, mangy and filthy, scrabbling about in the blood and bits of fur and small scraps of meat on the road, growling in their throats as they ripped pieces of skin and flesh from the doe. Bones cracked between their teeth, and it reminded Morse of when he was a boy and his old dog used to demolish the bones his mum brought back from the local butcher.

Wild eyes. Name tags on their collars. Claws that scraped upon the road as they pulled at the body. Their mouths stained red. One of them, an Alsatian, struggled to stand on an injured leg.

Florence stood close to Morse as he raised the AK-47.

"Please don't shoot them," the girl whispered.

A raggedy Doberman glared up at them, its big black eyes glazed with hunger and madness. And then, one by one, the other dogs turned away from the deer and began growling and snarling, showing their teeth and dirty mouths.

"It's okay," Morse said, without looking away from the dogs. "Don't run." He pulled her with him as they moved around the dogs, walking backwards with the rifle raised. Florence made small noises and held her hands to her mouth.

The Doberman stepped forward and sniffed the air. Opened its mouth. A glimpse of its lolling tongue.

"Keep walking," he muttered. "Don't stop."

"Are they following us?"

"Not yet."

"I'm scared."

"So am I."

Morse didn't turn away until they were out of sight and the dogs were left behind. He urged Florence onwards as they picked up their pace. They were half a mile away before the dogs began barking.

\*

They stepped off the dual carriageway and traversed a field then crossed a stream of grey water that soaked their feet and left Florence gasping with cold. They hid behind the thick weeds and grass on top of an embankment and watched the carriageway, but after an hour, when there was no sign of the dogs, Morse was satisfied they weren't being followed and they returned to the road.

"It's not the dogs' fault," Florence said. "They've got no one to look after them."

"I know," Morse said.

"Would you have shot them if they came after us?"

"I said I'll look after you. I made a promise."

"No one keeps *all* their promises, Morse."

"I'll keep this one."

"Okay then." She glanced at him. "Morse…"

"What?"

"Thank you."

He snorted. "No worries. Keep walking."

\*

Specks of rain started to fall. Morse swore under his breath and looked at the sky. In the west, echoing detonations of thunder and sounds like falling rocks on a mountainside. He thought he could hear the sea to the east, but he couldn't see it past the dense treeline on the horizon. The smell of ash in the air made him think of firework nights when he was a boy.

He thought he saw the Burned Man watching them from the fields, and looked away. When he looked back, the Burned Man was gone.

By the side of the dual carriageway were the scattered belongings of refugees. Suitcases and bags. Children's toys amongst turgid weeds. A bag of golf clubs. A teddy bear so tattered and filthy it could have been a dead animal. He almost laughed when he saw a microwave in the long grass. A dismantled shotgun, ruined by exposure to the weather. All of it faded. And down the road a soft top sports car had half-mounted the crash barrier in the central reservation. A rusted pistol that looked like police-issue lay on the tarmac next to it. He kicked the pistol away and looked ahead to where the carriageway curved to the west. He hoped for no more dogs.

\*

# THE LAST SOLDIER

As they walked, Morse looked down and noticed spots of blood on the road where Florence had been walking. He halted and looked up. She was slightly hunched over and didn't seem to notice the trail of blood she was leaving.

His hand tightened around the grip of the AK-47. "Florence?"

She stopped and then turned around, and her nose was bleeding into her mouth and down her chin then dripping to the ground by her feet. A thin line of red ran from one nostril. Her eyes were glazed over, as if she was in a dream and that dream was of something kind and warm and comforting. Then she put her hand to her nose and began to smear the blood around her mouth like garish lipstick. And only then did she seem to realise what had happened and what she was doing, and she looked at her bloodied hand and began to cry.

\*

They sat on a suitcase by the roadside. After Florence's nose had stopped bleeding, Morse washed her face with some water and a pack of tissues he'd found in the glove compartment of a car abandoned on the verge.

Florence sipped water from her canteen and stared at the ground with glassy eyes.

"Are you okay?" said Morse.

"I'm okay. Bit of a headache."

"Just take it easy."

"I can't remember what happened, Morse. I was walking, thinking about those dogs and how they must miss their owners. Then I was bleeding…" She wiped a tear from one eye and made a puckered shape with her mouth.

"It's alright," Morse said. "You're fine."

"I'm scared. It was like I went away for a while. Somewhere else."

"Where did you go?"

"I don't know."

\*

Florence watched the sky as she walked upon the shattered tarmac. Morse watched her when he wasn't scanning the road ahead. He shivered at the faint gust of a cold breeze between the wreckage of smashed cars. A photo of a woman was taped to the window of a car and the elements had whitened it over time until she was nothing more than a slight apparition.

Morse stopped in the road and turned around. Looked back the way they'd come and squinted in the grey light.

Florence's voice behind him: "What's wrong?"

He didn't answer.

"Morse? What is it?"

He turned back to her. "We have to move faster."

*

"What is it, Morse? What is it?"

"Just keep moving," he said. "Don't stop."

"Is it the infected?"

"No."

"Then, *what?*"

"It's the dogs. Those fucking dogs."

They stumbled down the carriageway and when they turned the corner they both stopped in the road and stared ahead. Florence put her hands to her face. Morse stepped forward until he was beside her. Ahead of them, the burnt out ruins and ranks of vehicles filled both sides of the carriageway and stretched on down the road to the horizon.

"Do we have to go through all that?" said Florence.

Morse glanced over his shoulder then looked at her and nodded. "We haven't got a choice." He could hear the dogs far behind them; they were getting closer. "Shit. Come on. Stay behind me and stay alert."

Her eyes were damp and her mouth trembled. "Okay."

"They'll be some nasty sights in there, Florence, so I need you to be brave."

"I've seen lots of bad things," she said, and it broke Morse's heart.

He offered a wan smile. "Then you'll be okay. Ready to go?"

She nodded. "Ready."

"Good girl."

# CHAPTER SEVEN

Stepping between the ruined shapes of vehicles. The smell of melted rubber and ash, burnt plastic and smoke. Florence muttered something that sounded like a prayer as they moved between the blackened hulks of trucks and caravans. Morse had slung his rifle and now held his pistol in a two-handed grip, breathing lowly through the spittle-flecked opening of his mouth. His trigger finger itched and his blood felt hot. The stuttering of his heart in a palsied rhythm. His coat sleeve snagged on a piece of twisted metal and he struggled to pull it free.

Behind them, the sound of the dogs grew louder. Morse scanned the wrecks, his pulse quickening. He looked for movement in the maze of burnt metal. And to either side of them, among carbonised suitcases and belongings, the charred and disfigured dead dwelled in their tombs. Refugee families and desperate travellers. Morse looked inside the cars, and before he turned away their forms were revealed to him and the sight of them drained the strength from his limbs. Charred flesh melded to buckled sheet metal. Nightmare shapes with rictus grins showed their teeth, grimacing in the ashen light. Mummified figures in seats burned down to the frames. Hands grasped to doors or fused to glass. A scattering of rib bones around melted wheels. Ash beneath Morse's boots. Florence was sobbing quietly.

Children curled foetal in the backs of cars, scorched to black. Flaking ash and skin. Some still holding hands, siblings in death. Morse's throat thickened and his vocal chords closed up. It started to rain as he and Florence passed between the horrors, and when he looked into one car, he saw a small, shrivelled form in a baby seat. He glanced back and saw Florence staring. Then she turned away and carried on behind him.

Morse looked ahead to where the road curved away and there was no end to the lines of firebombed vehicles. The sight was enough to deaden his legs and fire jolts of panic behind his eyes. And as he watched, a blackened shape turned slowly in the back of a car and when its mouth opened the lower part of its face peeled away. Then as Morse watched, it climbed from the car like a broken puppet with crumpled limbs, all charred and brittle, its eyes blistered and white, and made a choking, tortured sound as it moved.

Morse swallowed down a vile taste in his mouth. The creature increased its speed until it was stumbling like a drunk and almost upon them. Its hands scratched at its throat. Bones moved under the papery skin. An awful, sickly scream rose from its swollen throat as it grasped at the air.

Florence cried out.

Morse raised the pistol in one clean movement and shot the blackened thing in the chest, and it fell back against the side of a car. It slothfully bowed its head to look at the bullet wound, and when it looked up again, lips wet with blood from its lungs, it came towards them once more.

Morse put one bullet in its head and one in its heart.

The creature fell into a tangled heap of scrawny limbs, and its suffering was done.

The barking of the dogs became louder, rising on the low wind. When Morse turned back they had already reached the first cars at the rear of the traffic jam. He looked at Florence and said, "Come on."

And then they were stumbling between the wrecks of vehicles and the bodies of incinerated refugees. One corpse was slumped against a wheel, its face seared down to the skull and the rest of it so much blackened rags and bone. An infected woman was melded to her seat, obscenely alive and wheezing through a mouth formed into a frozen gasp, unable to move anything except for her flailing arms.

The shattered tarmac turned to damp powder and ash beneath their feet. Motes of it rose into the air; it scratched at their throats.

Then Morse stopped. He looked ahead. Florence ran into the back of him. About thirty yards ahead, a large group of infected emerged from between the burnt out vehicles further up the carriageway. They were heading towards Morse and Florence and blocking the road with their number. Dozens of them. Filthy, terribly emaciated figures stalking between the charred shells of cars. They came swarming on raggedy limbs, quivering wretches with sickle-like hands. Soot-streaked clothes flapping at the movement of gangling limbs.

Morse looked back and saw the dogs running towards them, barking and snapping, hunting quarry across the wasteland.

\*

Morse fired into the infected swarm then took Florence's hand and pulled her with him as he moved towards the middle of the carriageway. The infected climbed over bonnets and squirmed between bumpers, wailing and screaming, pawing and scratching at metal and the blackened road. A tide of squalid bodies, implacable and insatiable, clawed towards them.

# THE LAST SOLDIER

Florence was close to crying and her free hand was busy at her mouth. The infected closed in. Morse fired blind over his shoulder and hoped to hit something. He pushed Florence before him and helped her over the crash barrier. She fell to her knees on the other side of the carriageway. As Morse was climbing over the barrier, a sniffling man skittered from underneath a car and opened his jaws to reveal needle teeth and a squirming tongue. His deranged mouth snapped at the air where Morse's foot had just been. But before Morse could turn the pistol upon the crawling thing, a feral dog came out from between the gutted vehicles and fell upon the infected man. Both of them tumbled away, locked in an embrace, the dog's jaws clamped around the man's throat.

Morse glanced back at the road and saw the dogs attack the infected. Savage mouths and claws, sprays of arterial blood. Arms ripped from torsos and bodies conjoined in conflict. Shrieks, screams and howls. Morse stared in some kind of awe before he tumbled over the barrier and pulled Florence along with him, and they fled towards the other side of the road to the cover of the knotted undergrowth.

*

They tore through the trees and bracken and did not look back, chased by the barks, howls and screams of fighting beasts. They ran until they emerged onto a dirt track and stopped to catch their breath, hunched over and gasping in the cold rain. Morse checked that Florence was okay; there were small scratches under her left eye and on her brow from thorns or bramble stems, but they had already stopped bleeding. She nodded at him and wrapped her arms around her chest. He looked around, heart pounding, and holstered the pistol. His lungs felt deflated and when he took in anything but a small breath there was a dull pain in his chest. He unslung the rifle and looked back through the trees to make sure they weren't being pursued. Nothing emerged from between the thin trunks, and he was grateful for a respite from the hunt.

They hurried down the track for half a mile until it ended at a gravel parking area where several cars had been abandoned. Beyond that was a graveyard, and a little further on a Methodist church older than the great oaks standing over the graves. It loomed onyx-black against the sky.

Florence pulled her coat tightly over her shoulders. "I don't like this place."

"We need somewhere to hide for a while," said Morse.

"But why the church?"

"As good a place as any."

"I once hid in a church. Frank took care of me."

"I know," Morse said. "You've told me before."

"Sorry."

"Don't be sorry. I promised to take care of you."

"I know."

Morse dabbed at his eyes with the heel of one hand. "Come on. Let's take a look around."

\*

They walked between the old graves, careful not to touch the decrepit, lichen-stained stones, and climbed the short set of steps to the arched double doors at the front of the church. Florence stood back, reluctant and pensive. She looked out to the graveyard and her eyes flitted among the resting places of the dead.

"Do you think anyone came here, even before the plague?"

Morse looked at her. "Why do you ask that?"

"Just had a feeling this was a lonely place even then."

Morse switched on the small torchlight attached to the AK-47. He opened one door then raised the rifle and stepped onto a flagstone floor. Shadows fell back from the light. The air was choked with dust that billowed in swarms and writhing clouds. The smell of treated wood, incense, varnish and old candle smoke came to Morse and reminded him of attending Sunday services with his parents when he was a boy.

Florence was holding onto the back of his coat, breathing in short gasps. They were in a vestibule, flanked by tall, black metal candle holders where the wax was burned down to wicks. Christian effigies, sacramental linen and deep shades of charcoal all about them.

Ahead of them, two banks of pews were cleaved by a narrow aisle. Grey light ghosted through the windows, where the pious faces of apostles, saints and kings gave little comfort to those seeking shelter.

Morse froze when he saw the figures seated on the wooden benches. He went to say something, but thought better of it.

The figures turned slowly to regard the visitors.

Florence looked around the side of him and did a sharp intake of air.

Morse counted five of them, scattered among the pews. All of them withered and mutated, burdened with severe injuries and ailments, slopping in the rags of their clothes. A ghastly congregation come to receive communion from the figure in the pulpit: a priest whose clerical garments barely contained the tumescent deformity of his body as he gasped and gurgled through a dripping mouth.

# THE LAST SOLDIER

Florence let out a deep sob.

Morse turned and pulled her towards the door when the infected began rising from their seats, huffing and rasping wetly while the priest shrieked his woes and lamentation.

# CHAPTER EIGHT

They walked a sodden dirt track under a sky heavy with cloud. Distant shrouds of rain swept each horizon.

"I haven't heard any infected, or the dogs," Morse said.

"Are we going back to the road?" Florence asked.

"Do you want to?"

"I don't know."

"That's okay. We'll just see where the track takes us." He checked his compass. "Keep going south?"

Florence glanced at him and wiped her mouth. "Yeah, I think so."

"Do you feel sorry for them?"

"Who?"

"The infected."

"Yeah."

"The people they once were are long gone; those things are drones. Mindless things. Meat puppets."

"I don't think that's true."

"What?"

Florence picked up a stone from the ground and held to her face as she walked, brushing away bits of dirt.

"You shouldn't feel sorry for the monsters," Morse said. "That's how you let your guard down and end up infected."

"I'm already infected."

"Not in the same way."

"Would you kill me, Morse?"

He stopped and turned to her. "How can you ask me that?"

She stared into his face and her eyes had a glazed shine to them. "Would you kill me, if you thought I was dangerous?"

"You're not dangerous, Florence. What's inside your head is different than the plague."

"So you won't answer my question."

"I thought I just did."

"It doesn't matter," she said.

"Would you want me to kill you if you became dangerous?"

"I think I would. I don't want to hurt you, Morse."

"You won't hurt me, Florence."

"You don't know that."

"Let's talk about something else," Morse said.

"Okay. Do you want to talk about football?"

"Not really. Let's keep moving."

\*

The wind wailed and rose and fell, then died to a silence so profound Morse felt like he and Florence were the last two souls on a dead planet.

They walked a narrow road flanked by old pine trees. The rain hung in the air and shrouded a nearby village beyond the waterlogged fields. Bullet holes in the road signs. A burnt out ambulance mired in deep mud at the edge of a meadow. Little else to see but the land slowly fading into the murk.

Past abandoned houses where the doors of some were ajar and cold shades waited in dusty rooms. Animal tracks and the faint smell of urine. Weeds growing through the cracks and holes. Paths leading into dead foliage. Some of the houses had collapsed inwards and there was little left but wreckage and brick rubble. Florence made a low noise and fidgeted with her hands when they passed the remains of one collapsed house with a skeletal hand protruding from the ruins.

A plastic doll's head impaled on a barbed wire fence. Rainwater droplets on dead leaves. Flapping rags in the hedgerows. Morse watched for shapes and shadows. When the breeze ghosted down bridle paths and old tracks it seemed full of frail voices Morse recognised, but he knew it was a thing of his mind and he would not be fooled. He sometimes thought he was going slow in the head and a little mad, but it was a concern he ignored for now.

They climbed a hill. Morse swept the countryside with the binoculars. Cold, grey land. Everything faded and dripping. Skeins of rain.

Florence stood beside him. "What do you see?"

He saw lone infected wandering the fields. Shambling figures without aim or reason. He didn't tell Florence.

To the south-west, near a copse of wiry trees, a pack of infected were hunched over something in the yellowed grass. Some animal they'd caught. Shredded tufts of fur drifted in the wind.

He didn't tell Florence about that either.

"There's nothing much to see," he finally said. He cleared his throat and spat.

"We have to go past the border and into England," said Florence.

"I know." He looked at the sky and screwed his face up. "We're losing the light."

*

Florence stopped in the road and pointed at an old billboard for Edinburgh Zoo. The billboard was tattered and faded, and the pictures of exotic animals were losing their definition. The girl stared at them for a long while.

Morse put his hand on her shoulder. "You okay?"

"I miss going to the zoo."

"I never really went."

"You never went to the zoo, Morse?"

"Not that I can remember."

"Can we go to the zoo? I know there's probably nothing there now, but…"

"But what?"

"I don't know."

Morse shook his head, wiped rain from his forehead. "I don't think it's a good idea, Florence. Edinburgh will be full of the infected."

She never took her eyes from the billboard. "The animals are probably dead anyway. It sucks."

"I know. I'm sorry."

# CHAPTER NINE

As darkness moved in they looked for a place to stay for the night, and when they arrived at a junkyard in the fading light Morse said it was as good a place as any other.

Florence agreed, but her eyes were nervous and she chewed her lip. Her face looked clammy and troubled. Morse led her through the large metal gates and between great piles of scrap metal and the husks of old cars. Engine parts stacked in skips. Derelict washing machines, microwaves and televisions, cast-iron sinks and truck exhausts. Splintered bits of furniture. Broken toys in black bin bags. Florence crouched and picked up a plastic dinosaur missing its tail.

"Tyrannosaurus Rex," she said.

Morse stood over her, glancing around. "Looks more like an Allosaurus."

"No, it's not, Morse. I've watched *Jurassic Park*."

She tossed the dinosaur away and it was lost amongst the anonymous heaps of plastic and glass. Then she stood and looked around. She nodded at a ramshackle hut further into the yard. Morse had already seen it.

"Do you think anyone lives here?"
"Let's find out."

*

The hut was empty but in disrepair. A slumped, squat shape. It looked like something cobbled together out of materials from the yard around it. Corrugated metal and slats of wood held together by nails and rivets.

The door was made out of overlaid lengths of timber, and Morse pushed it open and looked inside. A windowless space. A bed filled over half of the dirt floor. Stained sheets and an old pillow. But it was still better than sheltering under a tree until morning. In the waning daylight he turned back to Florence standing in the doorway.

"It'll do for tonight," he said.

*

They ate dinner by the light of a candle, sharing a tin of cold baked beans. They drank water from their canteens and listened to the silence outside. Florence sat on the bed and stared at the floor, lost in thought. Morse sat on a plastic milk bottle crate and watched her.

## THE LAST SOLDIER

She said goodnight and fell asleep. The sounds of her gentle breathing comforted him as he reloaded the pistol magazine and thought about the next day. He went through his nightly routine of checking the rifle and the equipment in his rucksack. He tested the pistol's trigger mechanism. Making work for idle hands while he imagined the moonless night pressing against the outside of the hut like swarms of beasts. And before he could dismiss his runaway imagination he fell asleep looking through the roof holes at the black sky that might not have been there if he didn't already know of it.

# CHAPTER TEN

"Lock the doors," her father said.

Florence stood at the window and watched Mr. Stewart from next door climb to his feet. Something black and worm-like was protruding from his mouth. He was trembling, and he pulled his hands to his chest and the fingers were crooked and scratching. He hunched over and began mewling, the skin of his face tightening over his skull. And when someone down the street screamed, he turned his head that way and took off with the most vivid look of hunger in his eyes.

Florence ran past her crying mother and up the stairs to her bedroom. She shut the door and went to the window and looked down at the street. People were running along the road, panicked and terrified. Among them were those like Mr. Stewart. They clawed and bit, scratched and mauled. Blood smeared on the road. Some people had fallen down. There was a baby's pram pushed over on the pavement. Spilled blankets and a pink rattle.

She saw Kieran Rose, who lived across the road, attacked by John Gorman and Patrick Loveland. He tried to fight them off, but they fell upon him and ripped his throat out and then began clawing at his chest to remove his heart while he was still *breathing and pawing at them in one last attempt to defend himself.*

*She saw Michelle Playle crouching by the side of the street, gnawing at her own fingers and staring at the sky.*

*She saw David Shires standing in his front garden, and the front of his t-shirt was soaked with blood and his hands were red. His mouth was moving.*

*She saw two little boys biting at a woman's pregnant belly, ripping at skin and flesh with quick movements of their mouths. She was screaming and spluttering, her eyes bulging with pain and fear. Blood on her lips. Her fingernails raking at the ground. The boys plunged their hands into the woman's stomach, and Florence looked away when they pulled out something squirming, grey and gore-streaked.*

*Florence moved away from the window and sat on the edge of her bed. She looked around at the posters of boybands and cartoon characters. Her collection of lava lamps. Her books and trinkets. She knew the world was ending and there would be no more school or gym lessons or shopping trips or chocolate cake because people were eating each other and there were monsters in the streets.*

*She cried as she heard her parents arguing downstairs. She thought of Mr. Stewart again; kind, generous Mr. Stewart, who gave her money to buy sweets and had fixed the puncture in the back tyre of her bicycle last summer. She thought of him and the people outside, and experienced a grief she'd never felt or had even known to exist.*

*There were more screams outside. She clasped her hands to her ears and began to rock back and forth, staring at the wall and wishing for everything to return to the sun-lit joy of that morning only half an hour before.*

# CHAPTER ELEVEN

Morse woke from a nightmare in which the Burned Man from his past roamed the back lanes of the countryside and called his name among the gathered oaks, birches, elms and willows.

He rubbed his eyes and sat up, grateful for the rifle next to him. The candle was burning down and the frail flame painted his silhouette on the wall of crisscrossed wooden planks and sheet metal. He yawned and looked towards the bed, hoping that he hadn't woken Florence. Then he froze.

The bed was empty.

*

Morse swept the rusting mounds with the torchlight. His finger remained near the trigger of the AK-47. The sky was all black and when the soft breeze fell in a certain way he thought he could hear distant thunder from the north.

Silence and spitting rain all about him. He crouched and put his hand to one of the small boot prints leading deeper into the yard between the amassed towers of junk and forgotten things. Then he followed the tracks into the dark.

\*

Past a jumbled pile of rusting washing machines and car engines, the torchlight revealed Florence kneeling beside a badly wounded infected man lying on the ground. The man clutched his bleeding stomach and wheezed into the damp earth; horribly mutated, with pulsing cysts and lesions on his deathly-white skin. His face was stretched over his skull and there were only sparse strands of hair left on his scalp. From within the dank hole of his mouth, a flesh-pink tongue swept across pale-slick lips. His clothes had been shredded to rags.

Morse stared at their pales forms. Florence looked up at the light and shielded her eyes with one hand.

"What are you doing, Florence?"

The man raised his face at Morse's voice and bared rotting teeth encrusted with grime and scraps of grey flesh. Florence placed one hand on his arm and the man looked at him and Morse thought he saw something like grief in his eyes. Florence nodded and smiled sadly.

"Get away from it, Florence," Morse said.

"He's in pain." Florence didn't take her eyes from the man. "He needs help."

Morse kept the rifle raised. His mouth opened, but he didn't know what to say.

"Please, Morse," Florence said.

He cleared his throat. "No. Come here. Now."

Florence looked into the torchlight, tearful and pleading. He thought she would protest, but she stood and walked to him, and only looked back at the infected man when she was beside Morse.

"What the hell were you thinking?" Morse said.

She didn't answer, because the infected man began to lift himself from the ground onto all fours and raise his head so that his face was vivid and appalling in the torchlight.

"He's sad and angry," Florence said.

Morse sighed. "He's a *monster*."

The man lunged towards them with his hands raised and his long fingernails raking at the air. He made it as far as two yards before Morse put a three round burst into his chest that, in the silence of the night, was like a trio of thunderclaps. Florence covered her ears and whimpered.

The man collapsed onto his back and his final breaths were expelled as his chest shuddered to a stop. Morse stepped away, his hands shaking, the smell of gunpowder acrid in his nostrils.

Florence looked at him and said nothing.

"We have to leave," Morse said. "The gunshots will attract the infected. More will be coming." He pulled Florence with him and left the dead man to the earth.

*

They stumbled through the trees. The infected screamed and screeched in the night. The woods echoed with high-pitched shrieks and the sound of bodies thrashing through foliage and bracken.

"Keep moving," Morse whispered, hauling Florence along, her frail form trembling in his grasp. Morse wiped sweat from his eyes. The rucksack on his back felt like a bag of stones he wanted to shrug off and abandon. He looked back and saw movement in the oily dark between the black trunks.

"Morse!" Florence screamed.

He faced forward as an infected woman bolted from the undergrowth, moving like an insect, filthy with dead leaves and mud on her clothes. Her pallid face bloomed in the dark and her mouth opened and she swerved towards them, her feet crashing through the grass. From behind her teeth, something emerged and split open and dripped.

Morse pushed Florence onwards. Then he halted and shot the woman twice, and she fell forwards onto scattered sticks and stinking moss. He glanced back to see fast-moving figures flickering through the trees.

He ran.

*

Through woodland and across open fields. The sky all dark. Morse's chest shuddered and he struggled for air through gritted teeth and rawness of his throat. Swearing under his breath and cursing himself for using the rifle.

The torchlight glanced across Florence's back as she ran ahead. The screams of the infected filled the night air. He shot two more squirming forms that attacked from his right flank and they flopped dead in the dirt. He pushed away the afterimage of their ravenous faces caught in the light.

Out in the dark, the monsters were gathering, drawn to the hunt. The sounds of bedlam out in the pitch black. Deranged cries and hellish shrieking.

Florence tripped and fell down. Morse caught up and helped her to her feet. She was sobbing, trying to catch her breath, her chest hitching as she stared into Morse's face with wild eyes.

"Keep going," Morse said, wheezing the words like an asthmatic. Pinpricks needled at the back of his thighs. Dull pressure at the base of his spine. Fatigue made his head heavy and pulsing.

He sent her onward and then pivoted as several infected emerged from the dark behind him like ashen ghosts. They sprinted and flailed. Morse took aim and scattered them with gunfire and they fell down and the darkness swallowed them again. He turned away and ran after Florence, following a collapsing wall, through puddles and boggy ground, wincing at the loud squelching of his boots. Ahead of him, Florence climbed over a low section of the wall. He went on. She was calling to him.

He was wiping sweat from his eyes when a spindly figure reached out of the darkness and leapt upon him, digging sharp fingers into his tactical vest. They fell together. The wind was knocked from him. He clambered to his hands and knees frantically searching for the rifle, but his hands only found mud and grass, and he grunted with panic until they finally touched the warm barrel and he scooped the rifle into his arms.

The infected thing, all hairless and thin, was already up and moving towards him; a lurching shape of gnarled skin and vicious movements. He drew a bead on the thing's chest and fired twice. The creature went down to its knees and gurgled then Morse put one round through its forehead and watched it crumple onto the ground.

# THE LAST SOLDIER

His ears rang. He shook his head. The pounding of approaching footfalls and damp, laboured breathing. Low growls becoming louder. Something like a pained, idiotic chortle drifted out of the night.

Morse took a kneeling position beside the wall and aimed into the loud darkness. His heart slowed with the comfort of the rifle in his hands. Sudden flashbulb memories of Belfast and Derry. A hymn before battle. Faces of the dead on the dirt they'd died upon. The cold ground of winter. Insults and threats mouthed by teenage boys.

The infected coalesced out of the dark, thin wraiths from the gloom, lurching, rasping and wheezing, drawn to Morse by their olfactory senses and the craving for tender slices of his flesh.

He was not afraid.

Flashes of lightning silhouetted the infected against the horizon.

The rifle barked in his hands, thudding against his shoulder, roaring fire. The rounds found their targets, piercing meat and shattering bone, until the trigger clicked empty and the barrel smoked. And then he dropped the rifle and drew the pistol and shot the last of them until they were all dead and there were just twitching bodies before him.

He stood, breathing slowly, restoring the air to his lungs. His arms throbbing. Something like joy in his blood. Exultation and euphoria singing in his heart. Sound and anger and screaming death. To kill, and kill well. The chemical bliss of killing the plague's children rose and buzzed, waned and fell until it dissipated in his veins like the comedown from a LSD trip. Then the shame and guilt gnawed at him, and he spat, wiped his mouth, his hands shaking with adrenaline. His teeth chattered.

Morse composed himself and reloaded the pistol then the rifle. He was climbing over the wall when Florence began screaming out in the dark.

\*

The infected man pinned Florence as she flailed and pushed at him. He tried to bite at her neck until he stopped and stared into her face, like he was suddenly beset by confusion. Saliva dripped from his lips.

Morse kicked the man in the side of his ribs and he tumbled away growling and ended up on his knees like some supplicant awaiting judgement. He raised his face and the skin rippled and began to peel back, and his skull split into a sharp-toothed maw that gnashed and spat yellowish fluid.

Florence scrambled away from the man. Morse raised his rifle. The white-hot rounds caught the man in the chest and throat, and he collapsed as if boneless into a broken heap, his diseased blood steaming on the cold ground.

Morse looked down at the girl. "Are you okay?"

She nodded and took his hand and he pulled her up. And then she hugged him tight and they stood in the field in the dark apologising to each other.

# CHAPTER TWELVE

They wandered the woods and fields until dawn, and by the time the sun was above the horizon they were exhausted and freezing, shivering in the new light.

The sky cleared. Morse couldn't remember the last time he'd seen the blue beyond the clouds.

They sheltered under a viaduct that spanned a train track. The steep walls of a gorge, overgrown with vegetation and dense vines. Huddled together and sharing food, their breath like mist. They didn't speak.

Despite the exhaustion pulling at his mind, Morse was jittery and wired on the last doses of adrenaline in his blood.

"Need to find somewhere not so exposed," he told her.

She looked at him, her face bloodless. Even her lips were pale. "Okay."

\*

They headed southwards, past the shapes of old towns. Refineries and haulage depots, factories and deserted roads. Immense warehouses on abandoned business estates.

The sun was pale white and weak. Seemed like such a paltry thing up there, a fleeting presence, as grey clouds moved in and blocked the light.

"Are we near the border?" Florence asked, trudging alongside Morse.

He looked at a road sign as they walked the wrong way around a traffic roundabout. "Still a way to go yet."

"I wonder what England's like."

"In about the same state of shit as Scotland, I expect."

"My dad always said they made Irn-Bru in Scotland. Is that true?"

"I wouldn't know, Florence. I preferred whiskey and vodka. And beer."

"Were you an alcoholic?"

"It's rude to ask that," said Morse.

"Why?"

"Because it is, that's why."

"Okay. But were you?"

"No, Florence."

"Fair enough. My dad only drank when the football was on the telly. He supported Arsenal."

"I can see why he drank."

"Did you support a team, Morse?"

"Yeovil Town."

"Who?"

"Exactly."

"Why did you support them?"

"I was born and lived near there."

"What did you do?"

"What do you mean?"

"When you lived there."

"Not much. Went to school. I joined the army at a young age."

"Were your parents worried about you joining the army?"

He sighed. "I don't know. Maybe. I didn't care at the time."

"Why not?"

"We didn't part on good terms. We used to argue a lot. I wasn't a good son."

"Why weren't you a good son?"

"I was always getting into trouble; fighting a lot and wasting my time. I did some stupid things that I regret. I caused my parents a lot of heartache."

"I'm sure your parents still loved you."

"Maybe," he said.

"Did you fight in any wars?"

"I was stationed in Northern Ireland during the Troubles."

"What's 'the Troubles'?"

"It was when two groups of people decided they really didn't like each other. It's complicated."

"Sounds simple to me."

"It really wasn't," he said. "A lot of people died. A lot of them died for nothing. Including some of my friends." He thought of the Burned Man following him through life.

"I'm sorry your friends died, Morse."

"Thank you. But it was a long time ago, and at least they never had to see the world end."

"Do you ever think about them?"

"Every day. But I forget their faces sometimes. If I saw them walking along the road, I'd know instantly it was them. But when I try to imagine their faces, they're just vague, blurry images."

"Sounds sad," she said.

"It was a long time ago. Worse things have happened since."

# CHAPTER THIRTEEN

After traipsing through thick meadows of dead ferns and long grass they arrived at the outer edge of a village. They crossed a stretch of tumbledown wasteland to the back of a house standing alone near the main road into the village. Morse broke into the house and searched the gathering of squalid rooms, relieved to find no infected or crazed survivors. They secured the building and holed up in the living room. Florence slept while Morse walked around the house. The driveway was empty; the former inhabitants must have left in the hope they'd reach the coast and be evacuated. He wondered if they'd made it.

He looked at sepia wedding photos and examined the small things that were once important to whoever used to live there. Ceramic figures and a dog bed. Trophies from the local football league. A photo of a middle-aged man in a tracksuit accepting an award for *Youth Football Coach of the Year*. Morse went through drawers and pored over junk mail left in a pile on a stool near the front door: letters offering loans and credit cards; a flyer from the local Christian centre; a birthday card. He looked at his reflection in a tall mirror and was shocked at the grey in his beard and the lines around his eyes. The dry opening of his mouth. Withering away like a straw man in the winter.

There was an impressive DVD collection. A games console that would have been brand new and gleaming at the beginning of the outbreak. A Dell laptop that he tried and failed to start. IKEA furniture. He noticed the door under the stairs and studied it for a short while before moving on again. A box of cheap jewellery on the dressing table in the master bedroom. Gaudy earrings and garish necklaces.

The bottom drawer of the dressing table was locked. He levered the crowbar between the drawer and the frame, and when it splintered open he stood back and had to sit down on the bed when the photos spilled onto the floor.

"Oh fuck. Fucking hell. Oh fucking Christ."

He had to look away from the Polaroid images of anguished, crying children clad in dirty underwear and rags. Tears and tortured faces. Being forced to participate in horrific acts. There were at least a dozen children, all of them pre-teen girls and boys. Some of them stared out from the photos as if silently pleading for Morse to save them.

Morse dropped the crowbar on the bed and put his head in his hands. Hard to gather air in his chest, like his lungs were flat with exhaustion. A wince behind his ribs, the reminder of his ailing heart. He made a low sound in his throat and screwed his eyes shut.

He took his hands from his face. He couldn't touch the photos. Then he stood, grabbed the crowbar and left the bedroom.

\*

Morse checked that Florence was still asleep before he went to the door under the stairs and found it locked, just like the dressing table drawer. He worked at the door with the crowbar and when it opened with a dull crack he stood in the doorway, coughing at the dusty air. He put away the crowbar and unshouldered his rifle.

The torchlight moved upon the walls of a small room not much larger than the inside of a telephone box. The smell of damp sawdust and mould. To his immediate left, a wooden stairway descended into silent darkness. Morse took a breath and the old air left a bad taste in his mouth. A feeling of dread seemed to settle on his shoulders and press at the back of his neck.

He pointed the rifle down the stairs, took the first step slow and careful, recalling when he was twenty and one of the first to arrive at a Belfast pub destroyed by an IRA bomb. The broken bodies and the screaming of women. The futile movements of the dying in the ruins. The heat of the fire. The last breaths of those pulled from the flames. Morse had held the hand of a man covered in burns and barely recognisable as human, screaming the names of his family until he'd died.

The Burned Man.

Such memories never went away. Such things were not meant to be forgotten.

*

He descended the steps. At the foot of the stairway he stood on the earthen floor and looked around, his eyes watering at the reek of decay. It was a basement as wide as the house with scratch marks on the walls of mildew-stained stone next to him. Cobwebs long abandoned by spiders. The far sides of the room were lost to darkness. Nothing moved.

He found the bones in the middle of the floor, formed into a pile and covered in dust. Children's bones. Two small skulls glaring from the dirt. When he crouched and examined the mound, he noticed teeth marks on several rib bones. A low groan escaped from his mouth, and he stood and stepped away, feeling the room move around him like a backwards carousel. He swallowed. Muttered under his breath. Slapped the side of his head until his vision settled.

He went on with the torchlight sweeping the walls. Short steps towards the shadows until they receded and he was standing before the bodies huddled together in one corner. He let out a sob as the light moved over the naked, dried-out corpses slumped over one another or sitting against the walls. Their gaunt, withered faces, stretched tight over their small skulls. Some of them had died embracing each other. The mummified dead. Stiffened limbs and paper-thin skin. The stink of old shit and piss forced him to step back. He counted fourteen bodies. They'd been dead for well over a year, he reckoned.

Morse turned away and returned upstairs.

\*

Florence rubbed her eyes and yawned. "What's wrong?"

Morse gathered his pack. "We have to go."

"Why? Is it the infected?"

"No. Do as I say."

"What's wrong?"

"Trust me, Florence. We can't stay here."

## CHAPTER FOURTEEN

They walked in silence, skirting the village and moving out into the fields. Florence didn't ask why they'd left and Morse didn't tell her. He stared ahead, lost in thought. After all the horrific and tragic things he'd seen over the years, he'd thought himself inured to it all; he'd been wrong and the thought of his hubris sickened him. He wondered about the names of the children who'd died in that awful, pitch black basement. He thought about that for a long while as he walked.

\*

Morse laid the map on the bonnet of a car mired in roadside mud, holding down the corners with small stones.

"Where are we?" Florence asked. She stood and looked down the road. Hedgerows flanked the cracked and crumbling tarmac. Yellow weeds. Sickly vegetation.

"We're near a village called Foulden," Morse said, checking the map. He took in the names of places and felt a sudden pointlessness to their coming here.

"Are we near the border?" Florence was throwing bits of gravel in the roadside ditch.

"Yes, we're near."

"How near?"

"Very near."

"Could we walk there today?"

"If we got a move on."

"I'm tired."

"So am I," Morse said. "Do you want to rest here for a little while?"

"No, it's okay."

"Sure?"

She looked at him, her eyes large and troubled. "I'm sorry about last night, Morse. It's my fault we were chased."

"It's okay," Morse said. He stifled a yawn and cradled his rifle. "But you have some explaining to do. What were you doing?"

She chewed on her lip. "I woke up last night while you were asleep. I lay there for a while until I heard the sound of an injured animal inside my head. Then I had an urge to go outside. So I snuck out and found the infected man. I wasn't scared of him, because he was lonely and sad, and he remembered bits of his old life."

"He *remembered?*" Morse said, unbelieving.

"Yes. His name was Darren Dilnott. He told me."

"He spoke to you?"

"No."

"Then how did you know?"

"I just knew. And do you want to know something else?"

"What?"

"I think he was glad when you shot him, because he wanted to die. There was still a part of his old self inside him, but it was overwhelmed by the virus in his blood. He'd seen himself kill or infect many people, including his loved ones, and there was nothing he could do to stop it. He was glad to die."

"Christ." Morse sighed.

"At least he's at peace now," Florence said.

Morse stood looking down at the road, thinking about the souls and minds of men, and hoping his own could still be saved.

\*

They walked for another mile before Florence asked for a break. Morse noticed a sign for a local flying school and they followed the dirt track several hundred yards through a ring of woodland that enclosed a civilian airfield. Morse thought there might be survivors holed up in the buildings, but when they reached the end of the track and saw the chain-link gate hanging open and rattling in the low breeze, he knew his optimism was misguided and he had to hide his disappointment from Florence.

They went through the gate, their boots splashing in mud and puddles, into the airfield. The wind slipped through the trees and the wire fence to sweep over large expanses of grass. Morse stopped and looked around. Florence was silent beside him. He led her to the control tower and the surrounding outbuildings, and they explored the silent rooms and climbed the stairs to the control room where they found the wizened corpse of a man in a shirt and tie and no trousers. He was still wearing socks. A leathery husk, like an effigy from olden times.

Nothing of use there. No food. Judging by the scattering of drawers and cupboards, this place had been looted a long time ago. Now there was just dust and decay.

Florence stood next to the dead man and looked at his shrivelled face and his empty eye sockets. She went to touch his grimacing mouth but withdrew her hand at the last second. She turned to Morse, her face unreadable. Morse offered her a weak smile and they went back outside.

# THE LAST SOLDIER

\*

They walked the weed-infested airstrip and wandered among the abandoned civilian planes slowly rusting into the sodden earth. Morse wondered how long they would stand in the cold and the rain before they collapsed.

Florence ran one hand along the bottom edge of a wing. Her face held a reserved sort of wonder. She glanced at Morse. "Could you fly one of these?"

Morse stood looking at the planes, the wind at his back like a constant follower. "No, Florence. I was a soldier, not a pilot. And I don't like heights."

\*

They roamed the empty hangars. Florence listened to her voice echo in the cavernous spaces and the sound of her footsteps bounce off the walls. Morse watched for infected, but there were none, and the only life they saw were the rabbits chewing on patches of grass near the asphalt runway.

When they went back outside Morse looked at the sky and tried to picture it full of planes and vapour trails. He hadn't seen any machines in the sky for at least six months. All the helicopters and jets were grounded or wrecked. The realisation saddened him and he looked away and scanned the fence around the airfield for movement. He spat, wiped his mouth, and watched Florence trying to get as close to the rabbits as she could before they bolted. When it began to rain they returned to the control tower and watched the downpour from the large windows looking out at the airfield.

\*

"I think we should stay here for the night," Morse said.

Florence glanced at the dead body in the chair. "What about him?"

"We'll have to move him."

"Okay."

"You take his legs."

They carried the body down the stairs to a utility room on the ground-floor. The body was loose and light in Morse's hands. Bones barely held together by sinew. Morse found a sheet of tarpaulin and covered the man and they left him there. Then they went around the building and secured the windows and doors, and when that was done they returned upstairs.

\*

# THE LAST SOLDIER

The light leaving the sky. The breeze sweeping over the airfield, pulling at the tattered windsock across the runway. It was getting colder. Florence sat in a swivel chair and flicked the switches on the control console. She spent an hour talking to non-existent planes and pilots over the broken headset she'd picked up from the floor. When she was finished playing, she just stared out at the airfield and the wide sky and said nothing.

\*

In the low light of the Coleman lantern, Morse checked the rounds for the AK-47 and the pistol, and then reloaded both guns. The task relaxed him and slowed his heart. Kept his mind distracted.

"How many bullets do you have left?" Florence asked, sitting across the floor, eating an MRE. Chicken teriyaki.

Morse put the back of his head against the wall. Sleep worried at his eyes. "Enough to make a difference."

"How many infected have you killed?"

"I can't remember."

"A lot?"

"Enough."

"Is it different than killing normal people? I mean, does it feel different?"

"Sometimes."

"I killed a man, once," she said.

Morse raised his face to her. "When?"

"A few days after the plague arrived. He wasn't infected. He was just an evil man"

"Why did you kill him?"

"Because he wanted to do things to me. He touched me and tried to kiss me, so I killed him with a knife."

"I'm sorry you had to do that," Morse said.

"It used to make me feel bad, but now I'm glad I killed him. Does that make me a bad person, Morse?"

"No," he answered. "Not at all. You did the right thing. He would have killed you otherwise. But he would have done worse things to you first."

"Yes, he would have."

"Exactly." Morse lowered his head and let his heavy eyelids fall. "Kill or die."

## CHAPTER FIFTEEN

Morse woke with a small cry and pawed for his rifle in the dark. He held it close to his body and waited for his breathing to slow. Closed his eyes and tried not to think of corpulent faces and rancid mouths. A memory of jaws biting near his throat and the bestial stink of the infected.

Florence's voice in the darkness: "Are you okay, Morse?"

He tried to speak, but he had no spit. He made a low noise, like the small whimper of a child, and then remained silent. Florence didn't reply. After a little while he heard her breathing regulate as she went back to sleep.

Morse looked into the dark for a long time and in his mind recited the names of dead soldiers he'd known in long ago years.

\*

They left the airfield behind and walked back up the dirt track and onto the road. The horizon was a thin red line slowly spreading into the sky.

"I think it'll be a nice day," she said.

"It'll be cold," said Morse. He watched the roadsides and the shadows under the trees. "You warm enough?"

"Yes."

"Good."

"How far from the border?"

"Not far."

Soon the sun was above the horizon. A thin glaze of cirrus clouds across the sky, blown by westerly winds. Morse would have called it pleasant in other circumstances.

Further on they found human remains. A spinal column, pelvic girdle, splintered leg bones. Morse located what was left of the skull scattered a few yards away in the dirt. Tufts of pale blonde hair. Scraps of skin and flesh remained. The brain, eyes and genitals had been consumed. The internal organs devoured too. An efficient eater had done this.

Florence stood staring at the remnants of some unfortunate soul. Morse looked to the ground around the chewed bones and placed his hand next to one of the large paw prints in the damp earth. The heel pad. Claw marks. Fresh kill and fresh tracks.

"What is it?" asked Florence.

Morse was thinking about the zoo advert they'd passed a while back. He hefted the rifle and stood, glancing around, watching the treeline.

"Morse?"

He looked at her. "The infected didn't do this."

\*

They walked the road, moving at pace.

"Maybe it was a dog," Florence said.

"That's what I thought," said Morse. "But the paw prints were too big. It was something large. A tiger or a lion. Or a panther or a leopard, maybe."

"A puma?"

"Could be. It was bound to happen when the outbreak hit. Some animals escaped from captivity."

"Do you think it's hunting us?"

"I don't know. But we're in its territory, its hunting ground, so we should get away from here."

Florence said nothing and moved closer to him.

\*

Two miles on, the road was flooded and there was no way through. Morse stood at the edge of the black water and tried to gauge how deep it was, but it was impossible to tell without going in there. And he didn't like the look of the water and what might be in it.

They would have to go around by entering the thick woodland either side of the road. Morse led Florence into the thin shadows away from the reach of the pale daylight. Under the canopy of wiry branches and dripping boughs they walked, stepping softly on the ground.

"Strange," Florence said, her feet crunching on leaves.

"What is?" Morse said.

"How peaceful it is. It's like the plague and all the death never happened. We could stand here and pretend none of it happened. And beyond these woods the world's still there, my parents are waiting for me to come home…and everything's fine. We could just go home."

Morse stopped. Looked at her, his charge. The frail little girl, her pale face framed by a plastic hood.

"That sounds nice," he said.

She nodded. "Yeah. But it makes me sad."

"I know. Me too."

"Really?"

"All the time."

\*

# THE LAST SOLDIER

They walked. Morse scanned the surrounding trees. Silence except for the vague chatter of birds in the treetops.

Florence pulled on his sleeve. Morse halted and looked to her. He raised his eyebrows.

She whispered, "I think we're being watched."

Morse kept his voice low. "Where?"

"Behind us."

"Did you see anyone?"

"A shadow."

"A shadow?"

"Yeah."

"Okay. Keep moving. Don't look back."

They resumed walking. Morse listened for the rustle of leaves and snapping of twigs.

"Is it the big cat?"

"Just keep walking."

Something moved in Morse's peripheral vision to his left, but when he glanced that way there was nothing there. The back of his neck tingled. His teeth began to itch. His fingers tapped on the rifle. Florence muttered something inaudible.

Off to the left was the rustle of foliage. Morse ignored it and kept moving. He tried to estimate how far to the end of the woods, but the trees seemed to stretch on for miles and thicken all about him. His hearing picked up the low sounds of the woods, the insects and the small mammals. The distant cries of birds. Florence's footfalls.

Something on all fours ran through the trees up ahead, across his line of sight, and vanished into shadow.

Morse stopped. Florence stood beside him.

A burst of laughter seemed to echo all around them, fading then growing louder and then fading again. Morse scanned the surrounding trees when he thought he saw a flicker of movement. Then the laughter came again, drifting from the heart of the woods. It was humourless and dry; Morse imagined it spilling from a swollen, dusty mouth.

Morse turned to his left when he heard the sound of snapping sticks and feet slapping on the ground.

He realised his mistake too late, and as he turned, a dark shape wearing a crown of sticks leapt from the trees to the right and fell upon him. They hit the ground together and the air was knocked from his lungs. The rifle fell from his hands and hung loose from his shoulders as the strap dug into the side of his neck.

The smell of old shit, sweat and piss assailed Morse as the figure grabbed for his throat with one hand while raising a knife with the other. Fetid, sulphurous breath blasted his face.

A bone-thin man in rags, face streaked with grime, his beard wild and knotted with filth. He was slippery and manic, scratching at Morse's skin like an animal in heat. Long fingernails raked down one side of Morse's face. He gritted his teeth against the pain.

The blade swept towards his throat and he barely managed to block the man's arm with his own. He grabbed his attacker's wrist and twisted, and the man shrieked but the knife stayed in his hand.

Morse twisted again, but the man craned his neck back and head-butted him in the face. He felt his nose bend, and tasted blood on his teeth. He slumped, disorientated, his vision blurry.

The man pinned Morse to the ground and raised the knife again; the glint of the blade next to his mad, filthy face. The hole of his mouth and the brown teeth past his scabbed lips. Mad sounds. The rattle of breath in his chest.

Then Florence appeared behind him and plunged a knife into his neck; and he froze as his eyes bulged and his face was all surprise and shock.

She let go of the knife and backed away.

The man's grip on Morse's arms loosened, he gurgled something like a question, and his mouth slackened so that it hung open and let out a small gasp. Morse heaved him away and stood, grabbed the rifle and stepped back.

He was lying on his back with his face towards the canopy above, the small slivers of grey daylight dappling his face. He shivered as blood poured from where the knife was embedded in his neck. He blinked, moved his mouth, but there was no sound. Then he reached for the knife and pulled it out and it fell from his hand. A kitchen knife with a serrated blade. Morse looked at Florence, but she only stared at the man, watching his life ebb away.

"He's not infected," she said. "They don't use weapons or wear crowns of sticks."

A trickle of blood ran from the corner of the man's mouth. His hands pawed weakly at his chest.

"Let's go," said Morse.

"Wait," Florence said. She looked past him, into the trees.

A woman stepped from the undergrowth, thin, animalistic and ragged. She stood over the dead man with her head bowed. She wore a composition of rags and animal pelts. Tattered trainers on her feet. Her hair reached down to her waist, knotted with bits of moss and leaves. She glanced at Morse and Florence then fell to her knees next to the man and enclosed his hand with hers. Finally she put to her face to his chest and began to cry.

Morse pulled Florence with him and they carried on and left the woman to mourn.

When they had walked ten yards through the trees Morse stopped. Florence went on a few steps before she realised he was no longer beside her. She looked back.

Morse was staring at the ground.

"She'll follow us," Morse said. "Come after us as revenge for the man's death. She'll try to kill us. I won't let her hurt you, Florence."

He turned and walked back to the woman. She was still kneeling over the man's corpse, crying and muttering. He hung the rifle over his shoulder then drew the pistol. Stood over the woman and the dead man. The woman glared up at him as he raised the pistol. His heart fluttered and he hesitated. The woman bared her teeth at him and spat. But when he noticed her other hand upon the swollen curve of her stomach, he lost the will to kill her and lowered the pistol.

"I'm sorry," he muttered. And then retreated and left her to mourn her dead mate. She watched him leave, her red-rimmed eyes watery and fierce. The last he saw of her was as she put her face to the dead man's mouth and kissed him.

Florence called to Morse from past the trees.

# CHAPTER SIXTEEN

They reached the edge of the woods and returned to the road. Just before dusk they found a bungalow set back from the road, down a gravel driveway overgrown at the sides with pale weeds that clung to their clothes as they passed. They stepped around the shapes of old bones. Florence looked back towards the road.

When Morse opened the front door he had to step back from the thick rot-stink of corpses. He told Florence to wait outside. Fixed a cloth over his mouth and nose then entered the building. He went through the rooms; human remains scattered everywhere, long-dead and decayed. Walls and floors stained with old blood that was almost black. This had been the scene of a slaughter. He touched one of the walls and ran his finger down a long vertical fracture that was crumbling at the edges. Mounds of damp plaster fallen from the sagging ceiling. Peeling wallpaper. He raided the kitchen cupboards and found a bar of Fry's Turkish Delight hidden behind a stack of greasy Tupperware pots and tubs. He hadn't eaten any since he was a teenager, and the sudden thought made his eyes watery.

Florence's voice from the back doorway startled him. "If we can't stay in here, I've found somewhere else we can spend the night."

He put the Turkish Delight in his pocket. "Where?"

"Come and see."

\*

They stood in the back garden as the light faded below the faint glimmer of constellations. The curve of the moon. The air turning colder.

Morse looked up at the treehouse nestled among the thick branches of a great oak, situated at least nine feet above the ground.

"That?" he said.

"Yeah. It looks like Bart Simpson's treehouse."

"We'll be cold."

"We have blankets."

"You sure about this?"

"Yeah."

"Fair enough."

\*

After pulling the rope ladder up so that no one could follow them, they prepared to settle down for the night. There was a homemade sign daubed in felt tip.

PETER'S DEN. There was a pile of superhero comics, and posters of Boba Fett, Darth Maul and Darth Vader loomed on the walls.

A small wooden desk on one side of the floor, beneath the glassless window. A beanbag seat. A shelf lined with old *Fighting Fantasy* books; they must have been passed down by an older relative, or bought from a charity shop, because they were the same editions Morse remembered reading in the early Eighties. They were collector's items with no one left to collect them.

In the desk drawers he found a Panini football sticker album from just over two years ago. That was the last ever season of professional football, or *any* football. There were also some plastic toy dinosaurs, a pack of pencils, and some drawing pads filled with sketches of fantastic creatures and cartoon characters. Peter had been a talented artist. It all made Morse very despondent and melancholy. He wondered if the boy was amongst the decayed remains back in the house. Then he thought it didn't matter because the boy was probably dead anyway, and that was that.

\*

In the low light of the candle, they sat beside each other and huddled under their own blankets and some Morse had taken from the airing cupboard in the bungalow.

The treehouse creaked in the night and the dark outside was absolute since the sky had clouded over. They had finished their dinner in minutes, ravenous as they had been. Florence's stomach gurgled as it went about digesting her food. Morse's legs and back were aching. They both stank. Morse had cleaned the scratches on his face with some TCP. He supposed he should be worried about catching an infection from the man's filthy fingernails, but it was something he could push to the back of his mind for now. His nose wasn't broken, thankfully.

"Where did you get that knife, Florence?"
"What?"
"The knife you used back in the woods."
"I found it in a house."
"I thought so."
"Are you annoyed with me?"
"No. I'm glad you did it."
"Oh."
"Thank you, Florence."
"For what?"
"For using it."
"That's okay."
"You did well."
"Do you think I could be a soldier?"
He looked at her and smiled. "Maybe one day."

"I don't think there'll be anything left one day. Not of people, anyway."

"You could be right," Morse said.

# CHAPTER SEVENTEEN

In the morning they climbed down from the treehouse and started towards the border.

They passed a stretch of grassland where there had once been a refugee encampment. Florence stopped to look, even when Morse urged her onwards, and in the end he had to go back for her. He stood beside the girl. She was biting one fingernail.

"You okay?" said Morse.

"Yeah."

"Best we don't stop."

"I know." She sighed. "The people who stayed here, trying to survive… they didn't stand a chance, did they?"

Morse looked out towards the ruins of shredded, tattered tents slowly being consumed by the overgrown grass. The site had already been picked through and looted, he reckoned. There would just be bones.

"It wasn't a good place to set up camp," Morse said, speaking to himself more than Florence. "Stupid, really. Out in the open, exposed on all sides. Indefensible."

"They must have been desperate."

"Yeah. Everyone was back then."

Florence said, "It would have been a few days after the start of the outbreak. A few families, on the run, trying to hide. Low on food and supplies. Nowhere else to go." She crouched and picked up a Lego brick from the grass by her feet. She stood and examined it in her hand. "The infected came from the west. A flock, most probably, full of the recently-turned. I think they came upon the camp at night while most of the people were asleep. They swarmed through the tents. People were killed in their sleeping bags. Children and babies crying. Screaming. A few of the men tried to fight with cricket bats and wooden clubs, but they were slaughtered and it was over in minutes. Some of the refugees were infected and absorbed into the flock; the rest of them were eaten. Mainly the children."

Morse watched her put the Lego brick in her coat pocket. "Let's go."

"Okay." She looked back one last time at the ruins of the campsite and said something, but Morse didn't quite catch it and he carried on with her by his side.

\*

They reached one of the last villages before the border and found it in ruins, save for a few cottages left emptied and looted, and most of those were burnt inside and hollowed out by fire. There was nothing to be found in this silent, desolate place. Crows perched on exposed beams beyond collapsed roofs. Woodpigeons in the charred trees. Graffiti had been scrawled on walls: **KILL THE INFECTED!!!! ONCE BITTEN TWICE SHY THEN YOU DIE!** *GOD HAS BETRAYED US!* And finally: **THESE ARE THE DAYS OF THE LAST PLAGUE**. The road they walked was topped with a thin layer of ash that shifted in the breeze. Morse pulled up his cloth mask and watched the ruins for movement.

A large rat ran across the road and vanished beneath the remains of a car half-buried by fallen rubble.

"It smells of shit around here," Florence said, covering her nose with her hand.

"Just keep walking. We'll pass through soon enough."

Another rat appeared on the same side of the road as the first one. It stopped in the middle of the road and regarded them as they halted. Morse raised the rifle. The rat watched them with black beady eyes and only moved when it caught scent of something on the wind and bolted into the ruined houses on the other side of the street.

And before Morse and Florence could move, more rats appeared out of the ruins and followed the two scouts across the road. Dozens of them, from runts the size of average rats to ones as big as the first scout.

Florence stepped back. Morse put his hand on her shoulder.

"It's okay," he said. "I don't think they're interested in us. They've got plenty to eat."

"Are you sure?"

"No."

"That doesn't make me feel better."

"Sorry."

The swarm crossed the road and disappeared into what was left of the houses.

Morse shook his head. "There go the inheritors of the earth."

Florence moved her gaze from where the rats had vanished. "I've never liked rats."

"They're not so bad. They'd have only attacked us if we were badly injured."

"Really?"

"Probably."

"Oh."

\*

The border country. Cold wind gusting down the road. Birds in the bare trees.

A mile outside the village, flakes of ash began to fall from the sky. They stopped. Morse held out his hand and watched a flake land on his palm. Then he brushed it off with his other hand and looked at Florence. She was frowning.

"I remember a few years ago," said Morse. "A volcano in Iceland blew its top.

Florence pulled her dust mask up. "I don't remember that."

"You would have been too young to remember."

"What happened?"

"It created a giant ash cloud in the sky and grounded a lot of planes at the airports. Too dangerous to fly."

"Did anyone die?"

"I don't think so. But it pissed a lot of people off. Some people couldn't go on their holidays."

"So you think this ash is from a volcano? Maybe the same one?"

He looked at the sky. Endless grey. He wiped his brow. "I think the ash is from somewhere else. Something else. But it doesn't matter now."

"You think it might be from a nuclear bomb?"

"I doubt it."

"Why?"

"I just do."

"You don't know then."

He looked away and thought about nuclear warheads detonating over cities of swarming infected. Mushroom clouds rising from black horizons. He realised it was already too late for them if the ash was radioactive.

They walked on.

\*

Further on, Florence found a deflated football and was kicking it through the grass at the roadside when she stopped and looked down at the ground. She gestured for Morse to come over and he went to her and saw she was standing before a steel animal trap hidden in the weeds, set and primed. Florence paled and looked at Morse, and he pulled her away from the trap and they carried on down the road

\*

Florence stopped in the road and put her hands to her face. She hunched over, and when she took her hands away there were smears of blood on her fingers. She raised the cloth mask to her nose. The bleeding wasn't severe, but it didn't take long for the cloth to darken with her leakage. Her hands shook. The blood around her mouth and down her chin gave her the appearance of a melancholy cannibal girl.

Morse watched the blood drip onto the road. Dots of red on the tarmac. He looked at her waxen face.

She put one hand to her head. Her voice was small and pained. "It hurts. Inside."

Morse guided her to the side of the road and they sat on the grass verge. Bloodied and trembling, Florence seemed frail enough to disperse in the wind. Morse put his arm around her and she rested her head on his chest. Her nose had stopped bleeding. The ash fell like the severed wings of insects.

Florence whispered, "I can hear voices."

Morse wiped ash from his face. "The infected?"

"The Plague Gods." She raised her face towards the clouds.

"What are they saying?" Morse asked.

She let out a drawled breath. "I'm not sure. Sounds like plans and schemes." She sipped water from her canteen. She bowed her head and sobbed in her throat.

Morse pulled her tight to him. He said nothing.

"I don't feel very well, Morse."

He just held her, and they sat while they watched the ash fall upon the scarred land.

# CHAPTER EIGHTEEN

Morse took her to the nearest house. She wasn't capable of making the border before dark, and it was already mid-afternoon. The hours seemed to fall away and the daylight was a mere glimmered respite between each night.

He searched and secured the house then brought Florence inside and lay her on the threadbare sofa in the living room whose walls were covered in framed photos of smiling people. He washed the blood from her face as she shivered under the blankets, eyes fluttering as she muttered the names of people she'd spoken of before. Then she went silent.

Morse watched her for a long while until she fell into a deep sleep.

\*

With darkness approaching he went outside into the falling ash and looked at the dimming landscape. He thought of the fields strewn with bones, slowly being shrouded. The wind carried the cry of the dead world.

# THE LAST SOLDIER

Ash crumbled under his boots as he walked to the end of the pathway. He crouched, pinched some between his fingers and put it under his nose; it smelled of long gone days and bonfire nights when he was a boy.

He looked to the sky when the crash and boom of thunder filled the clouds above, and shuddered in his bones. He stood. A sense of biblical terror tightened his heart. Angry gods demanding tribute. The Plague Gods.

He went back inside and bolted the door. Florence was sleeping soundly. He watched her eyes move under their skin lids and thought he could hear her heartbeat. She was his last hope; once she was gone, they'd be nothing else left for him. And he knew what he'd do then.

\*

Morse spent the next hour walking around the house, checking the windows and keeping watch. His body ached and he struggled to keep his eyes open. The pounding of his tired heart.

He went into the study at the back of the house and stood amongst the clutter of someone's old life. The dead computer captured his reflection as a thin shadow without a face. The desk was piled with paper and books. He yawned, swaying on his feet, rubbing the underside of his jaw. His eyes stung.

The ash whispered against the windows. When he squinted, it looked like snow, and he wondered for how long it would fall. He yawned again. Hard to keep his eyes open.

He only meant to rest on the small couch by the back wall and take the weight off his feet for a moment, but soon after sitting down he slumped backwards and closed his eyes and remembered a distant time when he was safe and warm and didn't wander through ruined lands teeming with monsters.

\*

*In his dreams he looked at a sky-high sun so bright it was glorious and otherworldly. He was ten years old. A dream of a memory.*

*His father took him to the local steam fair held in a field not far from the village. He was fascinated with steam engines. His father was stoic and reserved, but not unkind. Always thinking about things, and he never said a word that wasn't needed.*

*Joseph Morse licked a Cornetto and looked at the grass around his charity shop trainers. There was ice cream on the tip of his nose. His father looked down at him and took a handkerchief and wiped Joseph's nose clean. Then he returned it to his breast pocket and walked on, and Joseph followed behind him, the ever-faithful son.*

*Steam and smoke. Tractors and machines. Raucous laughter from thick-handed, bearded men in plaid shirts and braces and boots. Beards and whiskers. Smoking cigarettes and wooden pipes. The grind and bellow of engines. Fat women chortling from behind deep fat fryers. Barrels of cider and ale.*

*When they passed the hog roast, Joseph could taste the cooking meat on his tongue, and his mouth watered, but it was quickly replaced with the smell of chip fat, toffee apples and candy floss.*

*The barking of a dog tied to a tree, wagging its tail in the cool shade. A bowl of water by its feet.*

*Travellers hawking lucky heather and wooden clothes pegs. Goldfish in polythene bags of water.*

*Joseph looked at the sky and it was all blue and never-ending. He smiled. The sound of a brass band playing a slow song. And when he turned away from the sky and looked for his father, he was gone, lost among the crowds, and the wisps of steam that danced like ghosts.*

\*

In the darkness Morse woke dry-mouthed and cold to Florence's screams. His heart was wild and aching. He sat up on the couch and only after he rubbed his eyes did he see the dark form of a hooded, masked figure stalking towards him from the open doorway.

Florence called out to him from somewhere in the house. The sounds of scrapes and collisions, grunts and shouts mixed with the smashing of glass.

Morse rose as the figure, which had the height and size of a man, lunged and thrust a knife towards his face. He dodged the attack and deflected the man's arm. The man's other hand, closed into a knotted fist, swung around and hit Morse on the side of the face. Morse stumbled back against the wall and dislodged a painting from its hook that fell to the floor next to him.

The man smelled of engine oil and smoke, and Morse thought for a second that he was a remnant of the dream. The holes in the cloth mask showed crazed eyes and a dirty mouth. Morse pulled his pistol from its holster and raised it to fire, but the man rushed him and pushed the gun towards the ceiling while the knife swung down in a narrow arc. And Morse moved his head at the last moment and the blade embedded in the wall. Morse threw two quick punches to the man's kidneys, and he stumbled back but pulled Morse with him and they fell down to the floor. The man's hood fell back and the cloth mask slipped from his face to reveal a visage of creased skin and acne scars as he flailed without his knife. Then he jumped upon Morse and tried to wrench the pistol from his hand. They rolled against the desk, struggling for the gun. The man's face came close to Morse's, as if to kiss, and his breath was like rot. The pistol slipped from Morse's hand and skidded under the desk.

Then the man's hands were at his throat, squeezing and scratching. Morse grabbed the man's wrists and pulled them away then raised his head, opened his mouth, and clamped his teeth around the man's nose and bit down with all the pressure he could muster. Skin tore. The taste of metal. Cracking, ripping cartilage.

The man screamed and his fingers dug into Morse's shoulders as he convulsed. Morse pulled his mouth away with bits of the man's nose between his lips. And the man fell to his knees, clasping his face, blood seeping through his fingers.

The man was still screaming through his hands when Morse gathered the pistol from under the desk and shot him twice in the chest.

A sound in the doorway behind Morse; he turned as another masked man appeared with a snub-nosed pistol held at the waist. Morse raised his gun and fired at the same time as the man, then fell against the wall, intense pain and heat in his side. His hand came away bloody. When he looked up, the man was on the floor just past the doorway. Even in the dim light, Morse could see the hole in the cloth-mask covering the man's face and the dark blood spilling forth.

Morse slumped on the couch and put pressure on the bullet wound. He cried out and thumped the seat of the couch with the other hand. The bullet had grazed the left side of his torso and missed his spleen by inches. Sweat beaded on his forehead as he tried to calm his breathing and the riot of his heart, and then he rose from the couch with the pistol in hand, aware that the house was silent, and stumbled through the doorway towards the front of the house.

He reached the front door and kicked it open into the falling ash and caught a glimpse of Florence being bundled into the back of a black van. When the hooded men around the van saw Morse, they raised their guns and fired.

Morse threw himself to the floor as bullets tore into the front of the house and the kitchen window shattered inwards. The wound in his side burned white hot. Then the gunfire cut out. The sound of doors being opened and shut. The growl of the van's engine and the scrape of tyres. By the time Morse climbed from the floor, the van was already halfway down the track and beyond his reach.

# CHAPTER NINETEEN

Morse cried through clenched teeth as he cleaned the bullet wound with a gauze pad from his First Aid kit, the taste of the man's flesh and skin still rancid in his mouth. Sweat dripped from his face. Sharp breaths taken and given.

He wrapped a dressing around his torso to cover the wound and tried to stand but his legs surrendered beneath him and he had to sit back down again. He grimaced, swore under his breath, and wiped his eyes. He had failed Florence, and whatever happened to her now was his fault, because he was incompetent and old and useless. Not fit to carry a rifle.

An old soldier too soft and slow to do his job.

\*

The men had taken all of Florence's belongings, even the blankets she'd slept beneath.

With the darkness of the house behind him he walked out into the falling ash, one hand at his wounded side. He had enough food and water for a few days.

Tyre tracks leading away from the house.

And there was movement in the dark about him.

Attracted by the gunfire, dozens of figures emerged slowly from the fields around the house, wheezing and growling, staggering like broken puppets. Deformed, gangly things on thin legs.

"Oh god." His voice was a weak croak.

The infected moved towards him, catching his scent, breathing in the musk of his sweat and failure. Some of them made snapping noises with their sharp mouths; others screeched and flailed their arms in agitation.

Morse spat bloody saliva from his aching mouth. His vision swam. The bullet wound throbbed hotly and he wondered if he would pass out before the infected fell upon him.

He raised the rifle, flicked the safety lever off, and sighted the nearest infected, struggling to keep his hands steady.

There was a last thought of his failure and Florence as the ash fell and the infected closed in.

He pulled the trigger.

The monsters screamed in their absolute hunger.

\*

# THE LAST SOLDIER

In the silent dark he limped and staggered onward, following the tyre tracks in the ash and mud. The rifle was lost back at the house, there were only a few rounds left for the pistol, and his knife was stained red in its sheath. He was covered in blood and gore, exhausted and shivering, each breath taken as if it were the last one.

How far had he walked? Hard to tell in the darkness and the raining ash.

A little voice in the back of his head said he should use the pistol to take the honourable way out, but he just shook his head and told the voice to go away. He would follow the tyre tracks to their end, or as far as he could go before he collapsed. And then that would be that.

He stopped and looked around. There was a road sign, but he couldn't read it because his vision was blurry and whiting out at the edges. He thought he might have a concussion from when the infected woman with the ruptured stomach had knocked him to the ground. And he swayed and placed one hand on a wrecked car to keep his balance. The ash whispered as it touched the ground. He was crying. Remember the dead and remember them well. Into the dark he said names he hadn't spoken in years. Flashbulb memories of summer days and teenage years spent trying to get a blowjob from Sarah Morton who lived down the road.

Morse laughed to himself and tried to carry on, but his feet wouldn't move because they were so tired and his legs burned with a deep pain, and he eventually slumped to his knees next to the car and bowed his head as if to receive a blessing.

All for nothing. Nothing at all. He should never have let Florence return to Britain. He should have kept her safe.

The ash fell onto his shoulders and stuck to the drying blood on his clothes. He listened for voices out in the night. He asked for help but there was no answer. Nothing but silence. And it was as he thought of lost friends and lovers that he collapsed onto his back and stared at the sky until he closed his eyes and welcomed the end of suffering.

# THE LAST SOLDIER

RICH HAWKINS

# PART TWO

# ENGLAND

# THE LAST SOLDIER

# CHAPTER TWENTY

When he woke flat on his back he gasped for water with guttural mutterings and whispers that hurt his mouth. He ached all over, every muscle, ligament, tendon and piece of skin sore and tender, like something recently born from a scraping womb. His stomach winced with hunger and it took a while to remember his name as he stared at the minute cracks in the ceiling. The last thing he remembered was collapsing in the road with the ash falling from the sky around him.

Coming from one corner of the room was some kind of light, maybe a lamp or a candle, but he couldn't sit up to see what it was. His slack tongue slid over his furred teeth when he tried to speak, and all he could do was utter a dry croak before he passed out again.

*

Slipping in and out of consciousness as nonsense words spilled from his mouth. Glimpses of other worlds through fever-dreams and shuttered nightmares. No concept of time. Nothing was linear or orderly. He thought he could hear his two ex-wives in the room, arguing about which one of them hated him more.

With his eyes closed, he tasted water on his lips, then in his mouth and down his throat. He gave his gratitude to someone he couldn't see. He remembered swallowing a pill, and afterwards he had fallen asleep and dreamed of deserted cities ruled from the sky by immense, tentacled monsters harbouring mouths the size of caverns.

When he opened his eyes, his mother was kneeling next to him, her face looking down at his pathetic form. She asked him when he was coming home, because she and his father worried about him so much and wanted to reconcile with him. She said she was sorry.

Old friends appeared, standing over him with accusations burning in their eyes. They were angry because they were dead and he was hanging onto to life by a gossamer thread. They were waiting for him to let go so they could take him away to the dark places where they dwelled. Then they left, shaking their heads at him, calling him a stubborn fool.

*"I'm sorry,"* he whispered, his voice barely passing his lips.

When Florence came to see him she crouched beside his trembling form and stroked his hair, but her affection turned into condemnation and anger and she began scratching at his face and screaming at him, demanding to know why he had let the bad men take her away.

Morse cried and tried to shield his face, and when Florence drifted away he called for her to return so he could apologise and make things right.

But she never returned.

And soon it all went dark in the room and there were no more visitors.

\*

Morse woke in a corner of a windowless room and sat up and immediately placed one hand to the bullet wound in his side. His vision blurred and turned his surroundings to water, but cleared when he rubbed his eyes and let them adjust to the dim light in the room. He was upon a mattress on the floor, with a fresh dressing around his torso. The roughly-hewn blankets that covered his stomach and legs did little to keep the cold away, naked as he was except for his old boxer shorts and socks. When he put his hands to his face it was tender and felt bruised. He coughed until his chest was sore, and in his mouth he could taste the bacteria on his teeth and under the grimy fold of his tongue. He looked about himself and felt a knot of panic in his chest when he couldn't find his pistol and knife. There was a cup of water placed beside the mattress. He looked at it for a moment then grabbed it and put it to his mouth but at the last moment he withdrew the cup and examined the water.

"It's perfectly safe," a voice said from his right.

Morse swivelled, wincing at his aching body and the throbbing bullet wound. On the other side of the small room, a crouching figure hunched over a steaming pot on a camp stove. The smell of something like stew or soup. His mouth watered and he tried to recall how long it had been since he'd eaten.

He noticed a bolt-action hunting rifle standing against the far wall.

The figure was side-on to Morse, but he couldn't see its face because of the hood over its head. He felt a frisson of apprehension and fear, and thought that maybe he was the final ingredient to whatever was in the pot.

Morse didn't try to move; it hurt too much. "Who are you? What happened?"

The figure stirred the pot's contents with a wooden spoon. "What do you remember?"

He stared at the back of the person's head. "How about you answer my questions first?"

The figure stopped stirring. Then stood and turned to Morse, and within the hood was a woman's smiling face. "You're right. I'm sorry." She was short and thin inside her tracksuit top and the fleece beneath it. Jeans and dirty trainers. Fingerless gloves.

"My name's Sadie. I found you. You were unconscious." She stood over him and lowered her hood. Northern accent. Yorkshire, maybe. Blonde hair that was almost white.

Morse tried to remember the time after Florence had been abducted. His heart quickened, and bile stirred in his chest at the memory of collapsing in the road after staggering away from the house. The bodies of the dead infected on the ground. The blood on his face.

"I heard the gunfire," Sadie said, crouching next to him. "I waited a while then went out to take a look. That's when I found you in the road, half-buried in ash."

"I can still taste it," Morse said, stifling a cough. "You carried me back here?"

"Dragged you, actually. Looked like you'd been in one hell of a fight."

Morse stared at his hands. "Something like that."

"Who were you fighting?"

"A group of men," he said. "They took a friend of mine."

Sadie frowned. "Who did they take?"

"A girl."

"Your daughter?"

"Not exactly. Someone I was supposed to protect."

"I'm sorry to hear that. Why did they take her?"

"Why else would a group of men want a young girl?" He let the suggestion hang and looked at the floor. When he thought of what the men would do to Florence, tears welled in his eyes and he felt sick with guilt and remorse.

"If it helps," Sadie said, "her suffering is probably over by now. I'm sure she's at peace."

"She can't be dead."

"It's probably better if she is."

Morse bit the inside of his mouth and curled one hand into a fist. He closed his eyes but all he saw was Florence dead in a field, left to be carrion for the scavengers after she was no longer useful to the men.

He opened his eyes and sighed deeply. His skin itched.

"It's okay," Sadie muttered, and her hand rested near to his arm. He pretended not to notice.

"Where are we?" Morse said.

"On the English side of the border, south of the River Tweed."

"Northumberland?"

"That's right."

"How long have I been here?"

"Almost a week. You spent most of that time passed out or babbling incoherently and calling out in your sleep. Did you have bad dreams?"

"I can't remember."

"How do you feel?"

"Like hammered shite, but better than I did before you found me."

She nodded, gave a half-smile. "That was a nasty wound in your side. Pistol round?"

Morse placed his hand to the dressing over the wound; it was sore and tender to touch, but nothing close to the agony of before. "Some bastard snuck up on me."

"Did you get him?"

"Yeah."

"Good for you. Luckily the bullet only grazed you."

"Still hurt like fuck."

"I can imagine."

"Thank you for helping me," he said.

She shook her head, her cheeks flushing reddish-pink, then glanced away. "No problem. I gave the wound a clean and slapped a new bandage on it, then gave you some antibiotics so you wouldn't get an infection. You're due for your next dose, by the way."

"You didn't have to do this," said Morse. He couldn't look at her. "You could have just left me to die."

"Like I said: no problem."

"What's in it for you?"

She smiled at him. "Well, I don't get much company, so I'm forced to seek out injured men on the roads and bring them back here so I have someone to talk to."

Morse frowned.

"I'm joking," she said. "I just did what any half-decent person would do."

"I thought the decent people were dead."

"You're a pessimist, I see."

"Not much else to be in this world."

"Fair enough. I'll let you ponder that while I dish up the food." She walked to the steaming pot.

"What is it?"

"Squirrel soup."

"Interesting."

"That's one word for it."

"Is it that bad?"

"It's not terribly good, but it's better than cat meat."

"Really?"

"More or less."

"Okay."

\*

Morse spooned the soup into his mouth as Sadie watched, and when he was finished he handed her the bowl and asked for seconds. She dished up some more. He got stuck into it, barely stopping to breathe. He thought it best to swallow without chewing once he'd noticed the small grey scraps of meat floating in the soup. It burned his throat but he didn't care because the warmth in his stomach was the best thing he'd felt in a long while.

Afterwards, he tried to get up, but Sadie eased him back down to the mattress and told him to rest. She gave him water and some pills. She placed her hand on his brow and frowned.

"You've still got a temperature. Rest up, Joseph."

His eyes fluttered. "How do you know my name?"

She stood and looked down at him. She smiled without showing her teeth. "You told me in your sleep."

"Oh. Okay."

"I'm going out for a while, to find food. I'll lock the door behind me."

"Why lock the door?"

"So nothing bad can get in here."

"Okay."

"Go back to sleep, Joseph."

*

# THE LAST SOLDIER

In dreams Florence came to his bedside and told him of all the bad things that the men had done before they'd killed her. Then her skin peeled away in wet folds and she became a raw, red-slick thing pawing at his blankets until he pushed her away and she fled to the corner of the room and began screaming into her hands.

He was crying when he woke.

# CHAPTER TWENTY-ONE

Sadie returned empty handed. Morse sat up and rested his back against the wall. She unshouldered the rifle and leant it against a stack of cardboard boxes.

"No luck?" he said.

"There were too many infected around. Did you get much sleep?"

"Little bit." He closed his eyes and let out a deep breath. His mouth smelled like a sewer.

"Bad dreams?"

"Yeah."

"Want to talk about it?"

"Not really."

"That's fine."

He opened his eyes. "What time is it?"

"Early evening."

"I can't stay here."

Sadie placed her hands together. Her knuckles cracked. A note of anxiety in her voice. "What do you mean?"

"I have to find Florence."

"She's dead."

"She could still be alive."

Sadie put the bag down. "It's unlikely. Even if she is alive, how would you find her? Do you know where the men took her?"

"No, but..." His voice died and he remembered the dream and Florence's screams from the corner of the room.

"You're too weak to go outside, Joseph. If you went back out into the wasteland in your condition, you'd be easy prey for the infected. You need to fully recover before you can even think about going out there. Give it a few days and then see how you feel."

"Florence might be dead in a few days."

Sadie's eyes never left him. "She might already be dead. There's nothing you can do about it."

*

They sat around a Coleman lantern and ate mushroom soup from paper bowls.

"Where are we?" Morse asked. "What is this room?"

"We're on the first floor of a supermarket, in one of the back rooms."

Morse wiped his mouth. "You cleared the building of infected?"

"Yes. With the rifle and a hatchet."

"Impressive. You can handle a gun then."

"I'm competent."

"If you can catch a squirrel you must be pretty good. You from out in the sticks?"

"No," she said, steam from the bowl rising before her eyes. "I'm from Leeds. Worked in a call centre. City girl." She smiled a small smile then spooned soup into her mouth.

"Wouldn't have guessed," Morse said.

"Hard to tell with some people. It's just nice to have some company. It gets lonely out here."

"You've done well to survive for over two years. Did you ever try to escape the mainland?"

She swallowed. "Me and my husband tried when the outbreak first hit. He died on the third day. I watched him get torn apart by a pack of infected that included most of our neighbours. I barely escaped."

"I'm sorry," said Morse. There was nothing else he could say, so he looked away and picked food from his teeth.

"What about you? How have you survived?"

"I managed to get on a ship and escape the country. Spent a while on a Royal Navy aircraft carrier, squeezed into a room with other survivors. Ended up in a refugee centre. Not that it was any safer, of course, because the fucking plague was everywhere."

"Did you have a family?"

"Two ex-wives, that's all. I have no idea what happened to them."

"No children?"

He shook his head.

She finished her soup and placed the bowl on the floor. "Me and Chris were trying for a baby at the time everything went to hell. Hardly seems fair."

"It's not," said Morse.

"Just another sad story, I suppose."

Morse nodded. "Soon there will be no one left to tell any stories." He put his empty bowl down and glanced at her, but she looked away and her face was tragic and pale in the light of the lantern.

*

Sadie changed his bandage, and her close proximity made him feel awkward and embarrassed. He didn't look at her, and when she finished she stood and walked away, and only then did he watch her.

*

Sadie locked the door and put the key in her pocket. She turned to Morse. "I'm going to bed."

He was picking at the frayed stitching in his jumper. "Okay."

"You should probably get some sleep too."

"Yeah, I will."

"Good." She went to her camp bed on the other side of the room. She took her boots off then climbed fully-clothed under the blankets. When she had settled and her head was on the pillow, she said, "I'll leave the lantern on."

"Okay."

"Are you alright, Joseph?"

"Just tired."

"Then get some sleep."

"Will do."

"Goodnight, Joseph."

"Goodnight."

*

There were dreams of terrible mouths and the indistinct figure of Florence calling his name. Blood greased his hands and dripped onto his bare feet. The weight of guilt was his burden to be carried. He saw the faces of people he'd killed severe with judgement and condemnation for his vile soul and the blackness in his heart. The slick-faced Catholic priests from his days as an altar boy, watching him and gloating; they told him he would go to Hell. They told him he was beyond redemption. No salvation for him. He could wish to repent with all his heart, but it would not be allowed because his soul was marked for another place, where the demons and sinners capered and wept, and that would be that for Joseph Victor Morse.

\*

He woke in the dim light of the lantern, breathing hard and sweating, tears from his eyes streaming down the clammy skin of his cheeks. The wound in his side pulsed hotly, and for a moment of heart-stopping terror he was sure that a sweat-slicked, porcine-faced Catholic priest was lurking at the end of his bed.

He rubbed his eyes and wiped them dry.

Sadie was standing over him, shivering in a t-shirt and underwear. He looked up at her and opened his mouth, but he didn't know what to say. She knelt beside him and reached under the blankets and started stroking his crotch.

"What are you doing, Sadie?"

She didn't look at him. "No talking."

Before he could reply, she took off her t-shirt then undid and removed her tattered bra. Her breasts hung loose and pale as she climbed under the blankets with him. Then her hands were at the waist of his trousers and pulling them down his legs. Morse was frozen, unable to react aside from the stiffening of his cock in her hands. She smiled at him and then her mouth was where her hands had been and she moved her head up and down until Morse was gasping and digging his fingers into the mattress. And when he was close to climaxing, Sadie removed her mouth, pulled off her underwear and slid on top of him and took his hands and placed them on her breasts. She moaned, rocking back and forth upon him, and closed her eyes and grinned. Morse held her breasts tighter, grabbing handfuls of her flesh, and she responded by putting her hands upon his throat and pressing until he couldn't draw air. Sadie's movements quickened as she neared orgasm, and when she came and released his throat, Morse came with her and they both cried out in the wan light, and then she dismounted him in silence, gasping for breath, her face glistening with sweat and tears.

Morse lay back and looked at the ceiling. He heard her walk back to her bed and slip underneath the blankets. He said nothing. She said nothing.

When he eventually fell asleep again, he did so with the maddening remnant of her scent upon him.

# CHAPTER TWENTY-TWO

In the morning Morse woke and remembered the night before. He closed his eyes and groaned and put his hands to his face. Flashbulb images of Sadie grinding her hips upon him, and the memory-feel of her clammy fingers upon his throat.

He sighed. His mouth tasted like bad meat. His back ached and the wound in his side felt as if it were being softly probed by little fingers. The smell of cooking food in the close confines of the room only made his stomach turn and his bowels loosen.

Sitting up, he looked towards the other side of the room. Sadie was already awake and dressed, stirring the steaming pot with a ladle. She raised her face and smiled at him. Her hair wasn't so unruly and scraggly this morning.

Morse tried to return the smile, but the muscles at the side of his mouth wouldn't move, and all he could do was look at her while trying to think of something to say.

Sadie rose with a mug in her hands, and she walked over to him as he tried to hide his discomfort and pull the blankets up to his throat.

"I made you some tea," she said. The dull light in her eyes made Morse's balls shrivel. He looked from her face to the mug and took the drink from her offering hand and nodded, muttering his thanks. She stared at him. He tipped the mug to his lips and drank, and she followed his movements with her eyes.

Morse swallowed. "It's good. Cheers." He was already worried he'd said too much.

"I'm sorry there's no milk in it; we ran out of the powdered stuff a while back. But I put two sugars in it. I've been saving the sugar for special occasions."

She flashed her teeth. Morse lowered his face to the mug so he wouldn't have to look at her eyes.

"About last night," he said.

"It was nice, wasn't it?"

He shifted on the bed. "Ah, yes." Only after he'd spoken did he realise how unsure his voice had sounded. He looked up at her and tried to keep the shape of his mouth neutral and flat.

A slight frown creased her brow. "Didn't you enjoy it? Was it bad?"

He took another sip and swallowed before his throat closed up. "Uh, of course I enjoyed it. To be honest, it's been a while since the last time. I wasn't sure it was going to work properly."

"It definitely did." She put her hand on his knee.

He moved his leg, but her hand went with it. Her fingers tightened on his skin. He tried not to look at her, even when her hand began to move up his leg and onto his thigh.

"I'm hungry," he said, trying to distract her.

Her face lit up and she pulled her hand away. "I'll make you some breakfast. There's baked beans and pork sausages. From a tin, of course. I hope you like it."

"I'm sure I will," he replied, hoping not to sound too enthusiastic. And when he looked over to her, she was staring at him above the steaming pot, her eyes wide and the curve of her mouth severe and pale.

\*

She watched him eat. He forked the processed sausages into his mouth and chewed, avoiding eye contact. When he finished, she took the bowl and then checked his wound.

"You're definitely healing, Joseph. Getting much stronger."

He looked at the floor, her breath on his neck as she wrapped a new bandage around his torso. "Good. I need to leave soon." As soon as he said the words, he knew it was a mistake.

She tied the bandage too tight and Morse squirmed, grimacing at the pressure on his wound. She stared at him, and he was forced to look at her, the closeness of her sorrowful eyes, and the accusation of her mouth. He could hear the shallow breaths past her teeth.

"You're leaving? I thought we had something between us."

He picked up his t-shirt and held it bundled to his chest. "I'm sorry, Sadie, but I'm not sure what you mean."

"Last night," she said in a wounded voice.

"What about last night?"

"Me and you, Joseph."

"We had sex."

"Exactly."

"It was just sex, Sadie."

Her eyes were downturned. Morse thought there were tears. Her mouth formed a sullen shape. "You think I'm a slut?"

He almost reached out to her, but thought better of it. "No, not at all. Why would you say that?"

"Because I gave myself to you, and now you're rejecting me. I've been alone for so long, and then you came along, but now you're leaving and I'll be alone again."

The sight of the rifle on the other side of the room pulled the air to the top of his lungs. He cleared his throat and swallowed. "Why don't you come with me, Sadie?"

She raised her head and her eyes glistened. Her mouth was slack and trembling. "I'm not allowed to leave."

"Why not?"

"I can't tell you."

"Of course you can tell me."

A quiver in her voice. "You wouldn't want to know."

"Fair enough. That's up to you." With a sigh, he stood and pulled on his t-shirt then strapped on his tactical vest. He was done with this place. Too much time had been lost. Florence needed him.

Sadie was scratching at her mouth and sniffling wetly. Her eyes found him, and he stepped back because they swam with pain, rejection and a little madness.

"I have to go," he said. "I've already waited here too long." He ignored the twinge in his side and straightened his spine. His limbs felt heavy and weak.

"You can't leave me," Sadie muttered. Her expression turned Morse's insides to slurry. "Not after what we shared."

"Let me out of here," he said, trying to keep his voice firm.

"The door's locked."

"Then give me the key."

"No."

"Please, Sadie. I don't want any trouble."

"Any trouble?" She let out a burst of humourless laughter, and her grin was thin and bloodless. "You should have thought of that when you were fucking me last night. I gave myself to you and you took advantage of me, and now you're just going to discard me. You *used* me, Joseph. You used me and fucked me and then tossed me away when you became bored. I won't have it. I won't."

Morse held out his hands in an effort to placate her. But her shoulders were trembling and she was breathing heavily and tears fell from her livid eyes.

"You bastard!" she cried.

"Please calm down, Sadie."

She rose from the mattress, her hands bunched into fists. Her mouth opened and she bared her teeth. A screech climbed from the base of her throat and she leapt at Morse and rained her fists onto his head and shoulders. He tried to fend her off, but she was strong for her size and her clenched hands found his jaw and nose and caused little bursts of pain in his face. Morse stumbled backwards then pushed her away, and she fell onto his mattress, but she climbed to her feet and came at him again, her face savage and hysterical.

When he pushed Sadie against the wall, the air was knocked from her chest with a stifled gasp. He'd pushed harder than he'd meant. She put one hand to the back of her head and collapsed to the floor, dazed and mumbling.

Morse kept an eye on her hands as he crouched and went through her pockets. And when he found the door key he stood and looked down at her while she cried and glared up at him with murder in her eyes.

"It didn't have to be like this," he said. "I'm sorry." But he could tell she wasn't listening, and no amount of apologies would suffice now. He had to get out and away.

Before he unlocked the door and left, he looked back at her as she sobbed into her hands. There was a muffled growling from her throat.

Morse apologised again and left her behind, and her cries followed him all the way up the corridor and down the stairs.

## CHAPTER TWENTY-THREE

He limped down a ravaged aisle of the supermarket, surrounded by empty shelves and racks, his feet kicking through the trash strewn on the floor. Cardboard boxes and plastic bags, tangled with empty tins and cans. There were stains he didn't stop to inspect.

Pausing only to catch his breath and rest the aching wound in his side, he struggled towards the front of the supermarket, squinting at the grey daylight through the intact windows. When he reached the deserted check-outs, he glanced back over his shoulder and saw Sadie emerge into the store with her rifle held to her shoulder. He stumbled faster, ducking as a bullet struck a support column ahead of him, and then peered over the end of a check-out.

Sadie was hurrying down the aisle towards him.

"Shit."

She stopped and fired again, and the swivel chair to his right was knocked flat.

He staggered into the open and headed for the doors, but when he reached them they wouldn't open. And he turned around as Sadie walked into view. She aimed the rifle at him as he ran to his right, towards the toilets, and stumbled through the doorway. He limped down a corridor, but it was a dead end. He turned back and entered the men's toilets, swarmed by the smell of stale urine and shit.

Hunched over panting, his hands on his thighs. The floor was stained and slippery. Nowhere to go, except for a narrow window high in the wall above the urinals. He wasn't sure if the window was wide enough for him, but it was his only chance, so he climbed onto one of the urinals. The fresh air against his face when he opened the window almost distracted him from the terror of the situation, despite the murmur and rattle of his heart. He pulled himself up and started to force his way through the open window. The frame scraped against his back and chest, and the wound in his side felt like it was ripping, but he kept going until the sound of a rifle being cocked stopped him halfway through the window.

Sadie's footsteps approached behind him and stopped. "Get down, Joseph. You're not going anywhere."

Morse shuffled down from the window and fell against the wall. Sadie's face stretched taut with anger as she stepped forward, just out of arm's reach. She was breathing hard and smelled of sweat and gunpowder. Morse didn't see the rifle butt as it swung upwards and cracked him on the side of the head. He fell at her feet and she stood over him. And before he could raise his hands to his face, she hit him with the rifle butt again and again until the world blacked out and the last thing he heard was her voice telling him he was an awful, terrible man.

\*

Morse woke seated on a plastic lawn chair with his hands tied behind his back. His face felt puffy and swollen. It hurt to move his mouth. A sharp pain pulsed at the back of his skull. When he scraped his tongue over his teeth, one of the molars came loose. He spat it onto his lap and it tumbled to the floor by his feet.

He raised his head, swallowing blood, waiting for the room to stop moving. Sadie was standing before him, the rifle in her arms. She was dressed for the outdoors, her stern face framed by the hood of her thick coat.

"I thought you'd never wake up."

"You're insane."

"I'm merely giving you what you deserve, Joseph. What people like you deserve."

"Do I deserve this?"

One corner of her mouth twitched. "I can't let you leave."

He snorted, looked about himself. "Obviously."

"I wish you could understand. You need me, and I need you. I'm sorry it's worked out this way. I thought you would be different from the others, but you're just the same. You're all animals. Beasts. As bad as the infected."

"What the fuck are you talking about?"

"This is an old land," she said. "An ancient island. Deep time. The gods of the fields demand tribute, and they will always be here, always watching, part of the land. Part of the earth."

"Just get it over with. Shoot me. Hurry up."

"I'm not going to shoot you, Joseph; I'm taking you to meet the god that I serve."

"What the fuck are you talking about? There is no god, just monsters."

"I don't expect you to understand."

He glanced around, sneering, and pulled on his restraints without success. "So, where is your god?"

She grinned below glazed eyes. "I'll show you."

# CHAPTER TWENTY-FOUR

Sadie sniffled and muttered as she pushed Morse down the dirt track towards their destination, pressing the rifle barrel between his shoulder blades. Her feet slopped through puddles and mud.

Morse glanced into the empty fields and shivered, bowing his head against the drizzle. He didn't look back at her.

Flecks of ash rode on the wind or fell onto the black water that filled the ditches flanking the lane. The sky lacked colour. It all smelled bad, like the world was decaying in the aftermath of so much violence.

Gravel crackled under his boots. The drizzle soaked through his t-shirt to his skin. His body, except for his bruised and sore face, was slowly turning numb. Between the chattering of his teeth he spat bloody saliva.

"Where are we going?" he asked her.

"You'll find out. Keep moving."

"You don't have to do this."

"Yes, I do. The time for pleading and bartering has passed. Now it's time for the tribute."

"You're going to sacrifice me?"

She didn't answer; her silence was enough.

"Why now? Why didn't you do this when you first found me?"

"Stop," she said, and he obeyed, cringing and drawing his shoulders in. He looked to the field to their right, blinking water from his face. About fifty yards away an infected man was sprinting across the barren ground towards them, cadaverous and rabid, the skin sagging from his bones.

The rifle cracked. The infected man fell down. Morse looked at Sadie as she turned the rifle back towards him. A wisp of smoke rose from the barrel.

"Nice shooting," he said.

"Keep walking."

He exhaled. "Okay."

"When you get to the end of the lane, turn left. Understood?"

"Yeah." He spat again and let the drizzle wash the phlegm from his lips. "You didn't answer my question."

"Which one?"

"I asked you why you didn't sacrifice me as soon as you found me."

He sensed her hesitation. The sound of her slow breath.

"I denied them to you. Because you're the first one I'd taken a shine to. I let my guard down and you took advantage of me. Then you rejected me."

"I didn't reject you."

"Yes, you did."

"I didn't mean to hurt your feelings."

She let out a bitter laugh. "I tried to save you, but you pushed me away. We could have been good together, but you ruined it all. So now you have to be offered up to the gods of the fields."

He thought about all that and said nothing then turned left at the end of the lane.

\*

Through a stretch of barren woodland, the air cold against his teeth, his boots splashing in puddles and slipping on wet moss. Sadie kept the rifle to his back and didn't speak, and the only sounds she made were the damp movements of her mouth and the scrape of her coat against the thin trees.

Scratching branches and sharp sticks. Dripping leaves. Stinking mulch and stones. Distant animal calls echoed through the woods.

"How much further?" Morse looked to the tops of the trees. His larynx was sore. In the pale light, he sagged against a trunk covered in slimy lichen. Sadie pushed him onwards and merely told him to keep moving or she'd use her knife on him and he would arrive to the gods cut and bleeding.

\*

Finally they broke through the trees into a large clearing of knee-length grass. The drizzle had become sleet, and it fell fast like it was in a hurry to meet the ground. Morse wiped his face with his bound wrists and stopped when Sadie tapped him on the shoulder with the rifle barrel.

"We've arrived," she said, her voice weakened with awe.

"This place?" Morse looked at her. They were both dripping and cold, but Sadie seemed unbothered aside from the twitching muscle under her left eye.

"Keep walking," she said. "You'll know when to stop. This is the place where you'll die, Joseph. Can you feel it?"

# CHAPTER TWENTY-FIVE

Morse halted a few yards from the edge of a large pit in the centre of the clearing. Sadie gestured for him to move forward, and he did so reluctantly, watching his footing, until he stopped at where the ground fell away.

He looked at what dwelled within the pit.

At least twenty feet down, the bottom of the pit was covered in conjoined bodies and limbs and faces. Infected people melded together to make a monster, writhing and flailing, wheezing through wet mouths and vertical apertures. A heaving mass of glistening, tumour-swollen flesh. Nests of eyes and grasping hands. Serpentine appendages and sprouting cilia. Blood, pus, and pale fluid. And when those damp, squalid and squirming faces looked towards the daylight and the two figures standing at the pit's edge, they opened their mouths in gaping, silent screams and the rancid miasma of rot and bad meat was pushed before them.

"My god," Sadie whispered.

Morse stepped back from the pit. "*This* is your god?"

She looked at him and raised the rifle. "Wonderful, isn't it? Such a beautiful thing. It's hungry."

"The infected are always hungry." He heard them pawing and scraping at the pit walls, dislodging soil and grit. "You've been feeding them?"

"Sacrifice. You wouldn't understand." She smiled thinly.

"So what's going to happen? You shoot me, I fall into the pit, and they get their lunch?"

"Something like that."

"Don't you understand what you're doing?"

"I know exactly what I'm doing. It has to be done."

"Why?"

"Because God demands sacrifice, that's why." She stepped towards him and forced him closer to the pit, until he was right at the edge and black soil was crumbling near his feet.

"Please don't do this," said Morse. "If you want me to stay with you, I will. I'll forget about leaving. We can be together."

She shook her head. "You're lying. I see the lies in you, Joseph. I see the deceit leaking from the corners of your eyes."

From the distant sky, the sound of thunder reverberated through the air. The call of the Plague Gods in the clouds.

The infected in the pit gurgled and cried, excited at the close proximity of fresh meat. Morse looked down at them. Limbs and hands flailed madly, clutching and slippery. Pale forms writhed like oversized larvae.

He looked back to Sadie. "Go on then. Shoot me in the head. Get it done, you crazy bitch."

She looked down the barrel at him. He had always imagined he would meet death head on. But he was terrified and didn't want to die. It wasn't supposed to end like this. And he felt a sudden aching despair inside him, because he would never see the sun again. He'd never see Florence again. He wondered if he was escaping one hell for another, for all the bad things he'd done.

The wail of the Plague Gods was getting louder. They would be the last thing he'd hear, and it saddened him beyond words.

Sadie placed her finger on the trigger.

He looked up the barrel at her face and thought about the night before and the sounds she'd made as they fucked. He spat and waited for the bullet.

He hoped to be dead before he fell into their snatching hands.

The clearing was silent. He ground his teeth and tensed his wasted muscles.

Sadie breathed out, her face slick with rain and exultation.

The Plague Gods wailed directly overhead; Sadie glanced up for half a second and Morse took his chance and stumbled into her with his head bowed and rammed her in the chest. The rifle fired near to his head, and he cried out as he spun around blindly. A moment of panic until he righted himself. The report of the rifle left an echoing thunderclap inside his head. His ears rang with the aftermath of exploding air.

Sadie had fallen, and before she could rise Morse kicked her in the face, and she dropped the rifle and rolled away close to the edge of the pit.

Morse breathed hard, gulping for air. He faced her as she climbed to her feet and pulled the knife from her belt. Her face contorted with anger and madness, the skin over her cheekbones florid and taut. She turned the knife in her hand then took two quick steps and lunged, swinging the blade towards him; he was too slow and her attack left a shallow cut on his left arm. He grimaced at the pain.

They faced off across a distance of a few yards. Sadie feinted with the knife and smiled. She was muttering mad things under her breath, the recital of a prayer only she was privy to; the insanity of a wretched mind hollowed out by isolation and loneliness.

She lunged again, the blade held out straight, and Morse side-stepped her and hooked his arms over her knife-arm, squeezing her wrist tight against his ribs. He cried out in pain as her arm caught the wound in his side, but he held her tight, even when her free hand curled into a claw and swiped at his face. He dodged her sharp nails and head-butted her when her face came close to his own, and she stumbled away clutching her nose, whining through her hands. She dropped the knife.

Morse crouched to retrieve it from the long grass then rose into a standing position with the blade held between his bound hands.

Sadie was on her knees, scrambling for the rifle.

He staggered forward with the knife held out just as she lifted the rifle from the ground and turned towards him, and he met her just as she raised the rifle, plunging the knife into her stomach.

She let out a small gasp, and when her eyes fell upon him in that small moment he felt sorry for her. An expression of sorrow on her face. Her mouth moved silently to let out a low breath.

"I'm sorry," Morse told her. "I'm sorry."

Sadie stumbled backwards with the rifle clasped in her hand and the knife stuck in her belly. She tottered on the edge of the pit, and Morse almost reached out for her, but then she overbalanced and tilted back and fell away from him.

Her screams were all he could hear as he fled from the clearing and back into the woods.

# CHAPTER TWENTY-SIX

The thunder in the sky. The falling rain and bitter drabness of the land in the terrible winter.

Morse cut the washing line around his wrists by scraping it over a piece of torn metal hanging from the frame of a wrecked car. He returned to the supermarket and scavenged what he could from what remained of Sadie's supplies. A few tins of vegetables and two of ravioli. Two half-litre bottles of spring water. A quarter-full jar of instant coffee granules. The Coleman lantern, two candles and a lighter. A blanket. He put on his tactical vest and the heavy coat over it then grabbed two sharp knives from Sadie's collection, tucking one into his belt and the other up his sleeve.

He put the supplies in a holdall and strapped it over his shoulders then left the supermarket in the slowly-dimming light of the late afternoon. The wound in his side felt like it had been stretched and opened. He checked the bandage, fearing the worst, but there was no blood, so he left it alone and hoped it would heal, given time.

Crows circled above the woodland he'd recently fled. He hoped Sadie had died quickly and without too much pain in her pit of monsters.

*

Exhausted, sore and downcast, Morse found his way back to the house of Florence's abduction. The last of the light was leaving the sky and the cries of infected swept across nearby fields in the growing murk.

The bodies of the infected he'd killed were sprawled upon the ground outside the house. Gunshot wounds and obliterated skulls, twisted limbs and torn flesh. Animals had been at the remains and scattered bones. He stepped over stinking entrails strewn along the grass. Bullet casings glinted like old pennies.

He found his rifle lying in a patch of weeds, broken beyond repair. His pistol was nearby, covered in dirt and ash. The firing mechanism was ruined and the top of the barrel was split open. Not that it mattered, because he had run out of rounds for both guns during his fight with the infected. His rucksack had been torn open and soaked in diseased blood. Everything inside was broken, slick with stinking fluids.

He threw the pistol into the undergrowth. His machete was probably lost beneath the infected bodies.

# THE LAST SOLDIER

The thought of searching for it among the cadavers filled him with lethargy and despair.

Morse walked to the front doorway. Bullet holes in the walls. The jamb shredded into splinters. When he passed over the threshold and into the small hallway, the smell of rotting meat and mildew was all about him. He picked his way through the shadows, his heartbeat juddering between his ears.

The two dead men remained where he'd left them on the floor. He searched their pockets and found a map of Great Britain and some sticks of chewing gum. He wrenched the snub-nosed revolver from the fingers of the man who'd shot him. Four rounds left in the cylinder.

Better than nothing.

\*

Close to dusk. He would have to stay in the house for the night. No other option, unless he wanted to walk in the darkness without a torch or rifle.

He pulled the bodies outside and dumped them among the remains of the infected out the front. Scavengers would visit during the night.

\*

In the gentle glow of the lantern in the living room where Florence had been taken, he sat on the floor, looking over the map he'd placed before him. He sipped water between mouthfuls of ravioli, aching and drowsy, and several times he almost fell asleep with the tin of food in his hand. The skin around his eyes and on the bridge of his nose was darkened, and whenever he touched it he winced and wished he had some alcohol or a decent cigarette to soften the pain with chemical distractions. His jaw clicked when he moved it to a certain angle. His nose didn't feel right. Bruises and lumps throbbed on his scalp.

The name of a village on the map was circled in red pen. Just over five miles away. He wondered what the circle meant as he ran his finger over it then thought about all the dead villages, towns and cities that now belonged to the infected. He thought about it for a long while, scratching at the skin under his greying beard.

No idea of the time, not that it mattered. How quickly you could adapt to existence without the aid of timepieces and ticking clocks. He finished eating and climbed onto the sofa and stared at the opposite wall. The rest of the night was spent shivering under the blanket, listening to the scavengers outside, before he finally fell asleep and dreamed of terrible things that he'd soon forget once he woke in the morning.

# CHAPTER TWENTY-SEVEN

He left the house at first light, the revolver in his cold hand, and as he walked the day took form around him. The paling sky, washed out and wide open.

He stopped to stare up at a row of giant wind turbines. They had ceased working a long time ago, immense memorials to human ingenuity left to fall into eventual disrepair. How long would they stand? Hundreds of years? Thousands? No one would ever know, because people would be gone by the time the turbines collapsed to the earth. No one would be left to witness their fall.

He saluted them before he moved on; it felt like the right thing to do.

\*

Morse occasionally stopped to rest. His aching body gave him no respite, but he walked on, watching the fields, the roads, the ditches and the trees. Birds took flight before his treading feet. The rustling of animals in thickets and stretches of undergrowth. The cold air on his skin.

He hid from flocks of infected that stalked the fields; cowering in ditches with the revolver close to his chest, ready to use it on himself if they discovered him. He would not be able to outrun them.

It rained and then it stopped, and then it rained again even harder than before. He sheltered in abandoned cars, slumped next to leathery corpses with rictus smirks on their eyeless faces. He found a naked man hanging from his neck on a high tree branch, his tongue lolling from his mouth and his eyes bulging. The flesh was slowly peeling from his bones. Must have been dead for a few weeks. Morse could smell him from down on the ground.

\*

Later on, after walking for the entire morning and some of the afternoon, he arrived near the village. He stopped in the road and looked at a road sign, grimacing at the pins and needles in the backs of his legs.

SHOTBOLT – 1 mile

Morse climbed the shallow rise of the land and at the top he looked down at where the valley fell away from him. He took the binoculars and glassed the dark shroud of the village, lingering on the shape of the church tower, where a St George's flag bustled on a white pole. Stretches of road visible through the bare trees. And in the silence, the sudden sound of an engine down there. Something running on diesel. The whine of a faltering accelerator along one of the roads, echoing around the buildings and the trees.

Then he glimpsed the black van on the main road leaving Shotbolt. It slowed as it neared the fenced-in property of a large white house just outside the village. The van idled at the tall metal gates until a man in a cloth mask appeared from behind a wooden outhouse. He carried a crossbow and raised his hand to the driver of the van then opened the gate and stood back to let the vehicle through. Once the van was inside, he shut the gate and looked out between the railings at the road before turning away and following the van up the tarmac driveway to the front of the house.

Morse's heart quickened.

He kept the binoculars trained on the van as two men climbed down from the cab. The driver tucked a pistol into the waistband of his trousers, went to the back of the van and opened the doors. He said something then gestured for whoever was inside to come out. There was nothing friendly about him.

Morse watched. "Come on, Florence. Come on."

A thin, pale man in a crumpled jacket emerged from the back of the van and stumbled onto the tarmac with a clear plastic carrier bag in each hand. The bags were full of tinned food. Morse's stomach groaned.

The driver stepped closer and looked like he was about to do something to him. The plastic bag man looked at the ground, head bowed, subservient. Then the driver pushed him towards the front door and they went inside the house.

Morse watched the windows, but there was nothing to be seen. Not even a glimpse of movement. Was Florence in the house? And if she was, what were they doing to her?

He shook his head to push away the insidious thoughts. Closed his eyes and gritted his teeth. The coldness inside his chest was paralysing until the feeling passed and he spat by his feet to clear a metallic taste from his mouth.

He looked at the sky and thought that darkness would soon fall, and it would hide him in the approaching night.

# CHAPTER TWENTY-EIGHT

Glimpse of the moon past roaming clouds, casting shadows from tall trees. The endless sky of stars. The cold crept into his bones as he crossed the road, glancing about him, the pistol clenched in his hand. He'd ventured through the village, where the houses were dark and deserted, and the gardens were overgrown and surrounded by collapsing wooden fences.

Just another dead village in England.

He'd seen no infected. Maybe the men had cleared the village. That would make sense.

Nevertheless Morse still moved carefully and quietly. A cold sweat dampened the insides of his clothes as he stepped past an abandoned car shunted to the side of the road.

The night was silent all around him.

*

Morse crouched at the tall chain-link fence surrounding the grounds. The fence was topped with barbed wire. He wondered if the fence and the barbed wire had been there before the outbreak, and if whoever had lived in the house had been concerned with security.

Lantern light in some of the ground-floor windows. Morse wondered how many people were in the house.

On the far side of the property, torchlight swept the ground. Vague outline of a man: a guard on patrol. Morse would have to move before the guard walked around.

He pulled the blanket from his holdall and stood on his toes and laid the blanket over the barbed wire. Then, gripping the metal links, he hoisted himself up the fence and onto the blanket and stifled a cry when one of the steel barbs protruded through the blanket and into his skin. He gritted his teeth and clambered over the fence, cringing at the creak of metal underneath him. He dropped to the ground, but he landed badly on his feet, lost his balance when he tried to crouch, and fell clumsily onto one side.

"Like a fucking amateur," he muttered, wincing.

He rose into a squatting position tight to the fence. Looked around, swallowing down his dry throat. His heart flinched at the silence. He took out the knife. Staying close to the fence he moved down towards the front of the property, where the guard was at the gates, pointing the torch out onto the road and the field beyond.

When he reached the outhouse he stood flat against the wall and peered around the corner at the guard, then drew his head back quickly as the torchlight swept his way. His breath caught in his throat. The light grew larger and brighter until he could hear the guard's footfalls. Morse froze as the guard appeared no more than three yards away at the fence, facing the same way as him. The guard was hooded, with a cloth mask covering his face. He stopped to check the chain links, turning his back to Morse and rattling the fence with his hand to test its strength.

The guard turned back to his patrol route just as Morse stepped towards him.

Morse halted, caught in the weak edges of the torchlight, heart leaping under his ribs.

The guard swivelled his head and the eyes within the holes of the mask widened.

Morse rushed towards him. The guard raised the crossbow from his side and Morse felt the *thup* of the bolt as it flew past his head. He raised the knife. The guard didn't get the chance to reload. Morse pushed him against the fence and thrusted the knife into his stomach, covering his mouth with one hand. The man bucked against him and Morse stabbed him again and again, feeling the cut of the blade through soft tissue and vital organs, until he slumped upon Morse's chest and his muffled, frightened cries faded into silence. His tearful eyes remained fixed upon Morse's face as he laid him down by the fence. Catching his breath, Morse crouched and pulled the mask from the guard's face.

Thinning grey hair. A creased, weathered face. He had killed an old man. He searched his pockets. A photo of twin baby girls sat in front of a photographer's backdrop, laughing towards the camera. The date in the corner of the photo was from over three years ago.

Morse put the photo back in the pocket before he could think too much about it.

He reloaded the crossbow and slung it over his shoulder, turned the torch off and put it in his coat pocket. After he wiped the blade of the knife on the grass he stood and turned towards the house.

\*

Morse moved down the side wall, his boots making no sound upon the soft ground. He stopped at the corner when the back door opened and threw a rectangle of yellow light onto the grass behind the house.

A man stepped outside, carrying a plastic bucket; he walked ten yards out into the overgrown back lawn and stopped at what seemed to be a pit dug into the ground.

# THE LAST SOLDIER

A wet splattering followed the tipping of the bucket into the pit. The man spat and wiped his mouth with his sleeve, then placed the bucket by his feet and began undoing his trousers. As he pissed he whistled a slow tune.

Morse checked no one was following the man out of the doorway and moved from the wall, stepping through the grass, breathing lowly. The stink of putrid shit and urine came to him on the breeze.

He waited until the man finished pissing before he grabbed him from behind, wrapped one arm around his neck to tilt his chin and with the other hand dragged the knife across his throat, cutting deep through the muscle and severing the windpipe. When the knife came free there was only the man's gurgling and the desperate scrabbling of his hands. Morse held the man tight until he stopped struggling, then pushed him into the pit and sent the bucket in afterwards.

# CHAPTER TWENTY-NINE

Morse stepped through the back doorway into a laundry room. An LED lantern glowed on the top of a rusting tumble dryer whose insides were stuffed with old rags. The boiled bones of a small animal piled upon a plate on a low shelf. He held the crossbow to his shoulder and moved into a corridor, stepping slowly and lightly, his heart pounding. He stopped and listened, and the house was silent as if there were only empty rooms waiting for him.

Down the corridor there were two doors set in the wall on his right side. At the end of the corridor was another door. He crept along the wooden floor and put his ear to the first door and listened. Nothing. The handle gave with one twist of his hand and he opened the door and aimed the crossbow into the room. He shrank away from a fetid smell that was like fruiting bodies of mould. A window looked out at the back garden and let the moonlight inside, and it revealed an old mattress on the metal frame of a bed in the corner. A tussle of stained blankets at the foot of the bed. Black stains where the wallpaper had peeled away. Dirty clothes piled next to the skirting board.

He stepped towards the bed and saw the bloodstains on the mattress. Other stains too, paler and more frequent. Under the mattress was a chamber pot. He looked around the room and didn't like what the walls told him.

In the next dilapidated room he found a young woman in a frayed nightdress curled up on the bed, her knees close to her chin, staring at the floor. Her mouth twitched below the dull glaze of her eyes. No expression in her moonlit face. The musty air was thick enough to impede him.

She didn't respond to his presence or the crossbow in his hands as he crouched next to the bed. He looked into her eyes and went to touch her wrist, but drew his hand back at the last moment when he noticed her bare arms were crisscrossed with scratches and her fingernails had been chewed to the quick. She was thin to the point of emaciation and stank of cheap aftershave and the animal sweat of men. Her stringy hair, matted with dirt, had been cut into ragged, uneven lengths by someone with no concern for how it looked.

Morse's eyes were drawn to her thighs, where dribbles of a pale fluid glistened. His heart sank. An incredible sadness opened inside him.

"Are you there?" he whispered. "Can you hear me?"

No reaction. Catatonia had hollowed her out. She blinked. And then Morse noticed the shackle above her left ankle and the chain that held her to the bed. The skin around the shackle was sore and blistered.

His throat stiffened with anger as he spoke. "I'm sorry this happened to you."

Her face, mottled with fading bruises, remained impassive. Into his mind came an image of Florence chained to a stained bed, and he bit down on his rage until one of his back teeth fractured. He shook his head and balled one hand into a fist then stood and grabbed the foul-smelling blanket at the woman's feet and laid it over her so she wouldn't be cold. Then he turned away and left her behind.

\*

He emerged into a kitchen area lit by two lanterns placed at opposite ends of the room and immediately noticed the cloth mask draped over the back of a wooden chair nearby.

A man was at the sink, his hands busy at his crotch. The splashing of water and slap of wet skin. When the man turned his body to one side slightly, Morse saw that his trousers were undone and he was washing his genitals with a flannel dampened from the muddy brown water in the sink.

Morse raised the crossbow. He let out a low whistle.

The man looked up, and his face was caught in mild surprise as the crossbow bolt speared his forehead. Blood began to dribble down the bridge of his nose. He dropped the flannel and collapsed with something like a tired sigh onto his front with his hand held to his crotch and his head to one side. His legs kicked a few times before he fell still.

Morse put the empty crossbow aside and took out the pistol and moved to the open doorway at the other end of the kitchen. The laughter of several men issued from deeper in the house. The clink of glasses. He thought he could smell alcohol.

Into another corridor. He stopped at the foot of a stairway when he heard a woman scream from one of the rooms above. She was silenced by the stern, drunken voice of a man. The sound of an open hand upon a face spiked the flow of blood through him. The woman was crying. When the man laughed, the woman began screaming again.

Frozen with indecision Morse looked towards the shadows at the top of the stairs. A faint light from under the door of a room. The woman sounded too old to be Florence. But maybe she was up there in one of the rooms, tied to the bed and out of her mind with terror.

His hand tightened around the revolver and he breathed through gritted teeth. His insides quivered.

He wanted to break something. He wanted to crush the beating heart of someone despicable.

What was this place? What the fuck was happening here?

With all his nerve he turned away from the stairs and crept into a hallway where a candle was burning on a small table by the wall. To his right, the hallway led to the front of the house. Across the floor from him, a sliver of yellow light appeared between a set of hardwood double doors. Raised voices and raucous laughter drifted towards him. The reek of cigarettes scratched over his teeth and tongue, reminding him of old cravings.

He crossed the hallway in three strides and halted next to the doors. Rage swelled in his chest and filled his throat. He peered through the thin opening between the doors into a large lounge decorated with the stuffed heads of animals on the walls. Candlelight and cigarette smoke. On the far side of the room, three men sat around a wooden dining table, playing a game of cards. He noticed their accents: a Yorkshireman, a Liverpudlian, and a Welshman. Like the start of a bad joke.

Morse watched them for a moment. Shaven heads and long beards. Tattooed scalps. He recognised the driver of the van, whose beard was the brightest shade of ginger he'd ever seen. An MP5 submachine gun was standing against the wall behind the men. Morse turned away and looked down at his hands. Four rounds in the pistol. It would have to do. There might be other people in the room, out of sight, but he would have to deal with that when the time came.

He listened to the men talk. They joked about the woman who'd been screaming upstairs and the last time they'd ever fucked someone who struggled so much. They laughed and smoked and drank from bottles of vodka and whiskey. One of them suggested bringing the guard in from outside because it was cold, but the other two didn't agree and said he could go out and join the old man if he was that worried.

Morse waited for them to talk about Florence, but they never said her name or even mentioned anything about a little girl.

They kept laughing. Morse watched, one hand tightening around the pistol grip until the thin muscles in his forearms were rigid.

\*

He searched the other rooms off the hallway and found them empty. He returned to the doors outside the lounge and listened to the men tell jokes and recite unlikely stories about their sexual prowess; about which female celebrity they'd like to have fucked before the outbreak. The Welshman said he'd seen an infected Helen Mirren in a town outside Manchester. The Yorkshireman responded by saying he'd killed an infected man who'd turned out to be Russell Brand. The man from Liverpool called them liars and said he'd seen that fit bird from *Holby City* tearing a man's stomach out with her bare hands.

Their voices were slurring. Delayed reactions. Hand-eye coordination failing.

Morse pulled back the hammer on the pistol. Took a breath. Clenched his jaw and stretched his neck.

In the upstairs rooms, the woman screamed again and then fell silent, and that was enough for him.

He pushed the doors open and entered the room, raising the revolver in one hand. The men stopped talking and looked up from their card game, slack-mouthed and frowning, their eyes dulled by intoxication.

A moment of complete silence.

With one tattooed hand the Liverpudlian went for the pistol on the table. Morse shot him in the chest; he slumped in his chair with a cigarette stuck to his bottom lip and fell forward onto the table.

"Who the fuck are you?" said the Welshman. The colour was gone from his face. Confusion and fear in his eyes. He was broad and tall, with a scar running down one side of his neck. Black ink on his knuckles.

Morse put one round in his face, and he tipped over on his chair, fell against the wall and then onto the floor.

The Yorkshireman almost reached the MP5 before Morse shot him in the back, and he collapsed as if his legs had been swept from underneath him. He screamed and arched his spine. Morse hoped the bullet had snapped his vertebrae as he walked over to him. The man tried to crawl to the gun, but Morse took him by the neck of his denim jacket and pulled him away, throwing him down on his back. The man was crying, holding his hands out, muttering for mercy in a pitiful voice that only enraged Morse. Pinprick pupils in bloodshot eyes. Several of his teeth were missing, and the ones that remained varied between black and dark brown. Healing scabs on his scalp. Spittle landed on his bearded chin. His frantic, terrified movements smeared the blood around him, and soon his hands were wet red.

"You took her," Morse said. "Where is she? Is she upstairs?"

The Yorkshireman spluttered through his tears and the pain of the gunshot. His face was pale white and Morse thought he would not be long for the world. There was no exit wound in the front of his jacket; the bullet was lodged in the flesh of his back.

"Answer me!" Morse roared.

"I don't know what you're talking about," the man said, his face crumpling as he cried.

"Don't fuck me around. Tell me where she is."

"Who?"

"The red-haired girl. Florence. She was taken in that van you've been driving. Was that her I heard screaming upstairs? If you've touched her, I'll cut your fucking balls off and stuff them down your throat."

The man's mouth hung open and his bladder let go. The front of his jeans darkened. His arms trembled and he held them close to his chest while he looked up at Morse.

"Fuck you, piece-of-shit motherfucker," he whispered.

"I don't have time to waste on you," Morse said, and shot him in the head. He dumped the revolver and grabbed the MP5 from against the wall. Checked the rounds in the magazine and looked into the sight. Felt the weight of it in his hands. It was fitted with a retractable stock; a small flashlight was attached to the barrel. Decent bit of kit. He'd never used one during his service in the army, but he would adapt. It would do the job.

He took what ammunition he could find for the MP5 and then looked around at the dead men. His ears rang and his hands twitched. Adrenaline fired in his blood. He took a few breaths to calm his heart. The smell of fresh blood and evacuated bowels. The stench of recent death was always the same no matter where he went.

Morse walked out to the hallway as feet thundered upon the stairs.

\*

He trained the rifle upon the foot of the stairway, and when a man in boxer shorts, bare feet, and fresh blood down his front emerged, he put him down with a three-round burst. The man was lying across the first few steps when Morse limped over to him, and he tried to raise the pistol in useless fingers, but Morse snatched it from his hand and then stamped on his face until his skull caved-in. When Morse withdrew his foot there was red pulp on the sole of his boot.

Switching on the MP5's torchlight, he climbed the stairs to the landing. The dust in the air scratched the lining of his throat. The thick walls muffled the sobbing from one of the rooms. He stepped slowly, sweeping the corridor up and down, checking the corners and recesses where someone could be hiding with a blade.

There were three doors.

He opened the first one and entered a bathroom. Nobody inside. Flaking walls and the cloying smell of damp within wooden panels. The enamel on the bathtub was tinged red in patches. Spots of speckled brown on the shower curtain. The toilet was full of scrunched up bits of tissue. Old stains on the floor.

In the next room he found a disembowelled woman on the bed in the corner. A candle threw Morse's shadow upon the wall so that it loomed over the naked woman like some demon-spirit. He stood by the bed and looked down at her. She had been strangled, judging by the bruises on her throat. Thankfully her eyes were closed. Her face was swollen and sore from the attentions of the men, and her breasts were marked with shallow cuts.

Blood soaked the bedsheets. Her intestines frothed from her opened stomach. The smell was horrific, ripe with offal and wet muscle. The knife, which Morse noticed on the floor, had been busy between her legs too.

Morse turned away and covered his face with his hands. A hollowing sadness ached in his chest. The back of his mouth watered with bile.

He covered the woman with a cotton sheet from the airing cupboard and left the room before the blood soaked through the fabric.

\*

Morse steeled himself for the next room and let out a deep breath before he opened the door and stepped inside.

A woman was sitting on her bed, chained to the metal frame with leg cuffs in the same fashion as the catatonic girl downstairs. Her arms wrapped around her knees, she was clad in a tattered t-shirt and men's boxer shorts. Cowering and frightened, but alive. And she regarded him over the tops of her wrists, her watching eyes starkly wide and never blinking. Her hair was cut short and into ragged tufts. One of her tearful eyes was severely bloodshot. Mascara, blusher and eyeliner had been applied heavily to her face.

When Morse took one step forward, the woman shrank away from him and bunched up with her back to the wall; filthy and suffering from malnourishment, thin shoulders and limbs. The soles of her bare feet were black with dirt.

Morse slung the gun over his shoulder and held his hands out. "I'm not going to hurt you."

She raised the rest of her face from behind her arms. Her dry, cracked lips looked painful. "I heard gunshots. Was that you?"

Morse nodded.

She glanced at his bloodied hands. "You killed the men?"

"Yes."

"Who are you?"

"My name's Morse. I've come here to look for a friend of mine. A young girl named Florence. Have you seen her?"

Her eyes were downturned. "I only get company when the men come to visit." She looked up and spoke with a tremble in her voice. "Is Freya okay? I heard her screaming."

"Freya?"

"The girl next door."

He hesitated, looked away.

"She's dead, isn't she?"

"I'm afraid so."

The woman put her hands to her face and wiped her eyes. Shook her head. "Those fucking bastards."

"I'm sorry," Morse said.

A wan smile on her face. A tear ran down her cheek. "So am I. She didn't deserve to die."

\*

Morse checked the other rooms and found no sign of Florence. She wasn't in the house. He was terrified she was already dead, that the men had finished with her before he arrived here and dumped her body in some foul ditch or in the waste pit out the back of the house. It was a struggle to ward away such thoughts. A vague discomfort ailed the left side of his chest, and it only faded when he slumped against a wall and took a deep breath.

He returned downstairs and found the key for the woman's leg cuff in the breast pocket of the Yorkshireman's denim jacket, then returned to her room. She watched him warily as he bent to free the shackle from around her ankle, and when he backed away and gave her some room, she was reluctant to move and her eyes never left him.

Her name was Violet.

*

Morse searched the grounds and the outhouse then checked the waste pit for Florence, but she wasn't there. She wasn't anywhere.

When he returned to the house he found Violet sat at the table in the lounge, drinking vodka from a shot glass and smoking a cigarette she'd stolen from the dead Welshman. There were two empty crisp packets and a chocolate bar wrapper on the table. An opened bottle of water. She had dressed herself in clothes she'd found. Desert camo combat trousers and thick woollen jumper. A fleece jacket. A pair of old trainers.

Morse went to sit opposite her, but his adrenaline sparked tremors in his limbs, and he had to stay on his feet, breathing rapidly, pacing back and forth across a few yards of floor.

Violet peeled the lid from a tin of baked beans and began scooping out its insides with one hand. She ate noisily. She was ravenous. Morse averted his gaze towards the dead men on the floor, flexing his hands in agitation.

She looked up from the tin of beans, with tomato sauce smeared around her mouth. "Did you place a sheet over Freya's body?"

He poured a measure of vodka into a tumbler then downed it and smacked the glass down on the table. "Yeah."

"Thank you."

"No problem."

"And thanks for getting me out of that fucking room."

Morse poured another shot. "Don't worry about it."

Violet glanced at the bodies on the floor around them. "I'm glad they're dead. Motherfuckers."

Morse raised his glass. "Here's to human nature." He threw the drink down his neck and grimaced. The burn inside his chest was something to distract him from his fear that Florence was gone for good.

Violet finished the baked beans and threw the empty tin at the dead Welshman; the tin bounced off what remained of his face and clattered against the wall. Then she took a pull on the cigarette smouldering in the rim of the ashtray. When she took the cigarette from her mouth she stared at its smouldering tip. "I haven't smoked in years."

"How did you end up here?"

"I was captured a few months ago. I was heading northwards – had nowhere else to go."

"Did you try to escape the mainland?"

"I reached the east coast, but I couldn't find any boats or ships. So I thought I'd see what happened up north. They caught me outside a small village. Took all my stuff. I was brought here with some other women, to service these brave men. What a bunch of cunts. Never thought I'd end up working in a post-apocalyptic brothel."

"Who are they?" Morse said.

Violet tapped ash from the cigarette and returned it to her mouth. She took a long drag and held in the smoke for a moment before she released it through her nose and she sighed.

"They call themselves the *Order of the Pestilence*. Some kind of paramilitary group. This place is just a waystation and brothel for them. They're organised, from what I've seen and heard."

Morse rubbed at his face. The image of Florence's face wouldn't leave his mind. His insides were full of loose parts. "There are more of them?"

"Not here. Not now. But I think they've got a base somewhere south of here."

Morse looked at her. A sudden flare of hope in his chest. "South?"

"Yeah. It's their headquarters, I think."

"Where in the south?"

"I don't know."

"Are you sure?"

"Yeah, I'm sure. All I know is it's a men-only club. Their doctrine says that women are inferior and only useful for menial tasks and breeding. I've had a few of them spouting this bollocks at me."

"A lot of cults appeared during the outbreak," Morse said. "I didn't think any of them had survived."

"They're persistent and well-armed," Violet said. "Is this Florence girl your daughter?"

"No. But she's as good as. Although I've never told her that. I was supposed to protect her. Now I don't know what to do. I thought she would be here."

She shrugged. "Don't be too hard on yourself. It's all fucked. There's nothing any of us can do."

\*

On their way to check on the woman at the back of the house, Violet halted by the banister at the foot of the stairs. Her brow creased as her eyes flitted around the hallway.

"What is it?" asked Morse.

"I thought I heard something," she said, her voice low and conspiratorial.

"Where?"

She turned and pointed towards the door under the stairway.

"Could be just a rat."

Morse stepped forwards while Violet stood to the side of the door ready to grab the handle. He flicked the safety switch on the MP5 then nodded at Violet.

She pulled the door open.

The man inside the cupboard space screamed and raised his hands in surrender. He blinked at Morse in the glare of the torchlight.

Morse's trigger finger tensed.

"No!" said Violet. "Don't shoot him."

Morse stared down the barrel at the man, who was visibly trembling and pale, with a butcher's knife in one small hand. A patch of white gauze covered his right eye. Tracksuit bottoms and boots. A jumper under a black body-warmer.

"Put the knife down," Morse told him.

The man crouched and placed the knife on the floor while keeping his eyes on Morse. Sweat dampened the gaunt angles of his face.

"It's Tomas," Violet said.

"Who?"

Violet stepped in front of the doorway and shielded the man. She faced Morse and raised her palms to him. "He wasn't one of them. He's a good guy."

"There are no good guys."

"Please, Morse, put the gun down."

Morse lowered the MP5. He looked over Violet's shoulder towards the man.

"Thank you," she said. She turned back to the man and they embraced. Morse watched, confused and irritated. Violet guided the man out of the cubby hole and smiled at him.

"I thought you were dead or you'd done a runner, Tomas."

He smiled back, but it faded quickly, and he looked warily at Morse as he touched the taping around the gauze patch and scratched at the surrounding skin.

Morse glared at them. "Is someone going to explain?"

"He was these fuckers' servant," said Violet. "No better than a chattel slave."

Morse looked at the man. "Is that true?"

Tomas nodded. "Yes. Yes, true." Eastern European accent. Polish, most probably.

"The men treated him almost as bad as the women," said Violet. "He was here against his will. He was the one who had to clean, feed and water us. Tend to our injuries after the men had visited our rooms. He was nice to me and tried to help."

Morse gestured to the gauze patch. "What's wrong with your eye, Tomas?"

Violet spoke for him. "The men caught him giving me extra food and they beat the shit out of him in my room, while I watched. They blinded him in one eye."

Tomas was nodding. "Is all true. Fractured socket and damaged my eye so I can't see. Bastard motherfuckers."

Morse remembered it had been Tomas he'd seen climb out the back of the van earlier that day, when he'd been watching through the binoculars.

"Are they all dead?" Tomas asked. "All of the men?"

"Yes," Violet said. "They're all gone."

A relieved smile formed on his face. "Good. Hope they burn in hell."

\*

Morse watched from the doorway as Violet and Tomas released the catatonic woman from her bed. Tomas had found the key for the cuffs in one of the dead men's pockets.

The woman said nothing while they moved her into a sitting position. She wasn't much more than dead weight.

"What's her name?" said Violet.

Tomas dabbed the woman's face with a damp handkerchief. "Karen. I don't know where she came from. She arrived here a month or two before you did."

"She can't be any older than twenty. Jesus."

"The Order men treat her badly."

Violet glanced towards Morse. "We'll get her dressed and sorted."

"Okay," he said. "I'll leave you to it."

He walked the corridors of the house for a while, looking for any sign of Florence. But there were none and he realised he had lost Florence for good.

# CHAPTER THIRTY

The constellations faded with the first shades of light in the sky. Fire bled upon the eastern horizon.

Morse stood on the driveway, arms folded over his chest, the MP5 hanging over his shoulders. His ears chimed with tinnitus. Beyond the perimeter fence, the village was silent and thin mist obscured the fields. He imagined he was the last person left alive in an empty world. It wasn't hard to picture on mornings like this. He'd read a book a few years ago, before the outbreak, about an astronaut stranded on Mars after his crew had left him behind. The book had deeply affected him at the time.

Loneliness had scared him all of his life. That and getting older. How many years left for him? How many sunrises remained?

*I'm sorry, Florence. I'm sorry I couldn't find you.*

He should have kept one of the men alive, for interrogation. But the anger and the urge to kill had swarmed his mind.

Someone approached behind him on the gravel. He swivelled his head slightly and placed one hand on his gun. Violet and Tomas stopped and regarded him. He turned towards them.

"Are you leaving, Morse?" Tomas said.

"Why do you ask?"

"We want to go with you," said Violet.

"We can help you," Tomas added.

"How?"

Tomas scratched his eyepatch. "Violet told me about the girl. Florence, is it?"

"Yeah, what about her?"

"She has red hair, right?"

"That's right."

"I think the Order brought her here."

Morse stepped towards Tomas. "You've seen her?"

"Yes, a girl. Red hair. I think was your Florence."

A frisson of hope in Morse's chest; a sliver of dread, too, at what the men might have done to her in this terrible house. "Did they put her in one of the rooms, like the women? Did they...?"

"She only stayed for a few hours and then some other men took her away in a car. I think I know where they take Florence."

"Where?"

"A place called Black Heddon. They have a base there. They told me this many times. They said I would have to go there one day."

"Where is this place?" Morse said.

"Many miles," Tomas replied. "But we have the van, so we can make it. I can show you on map."

"We want to come with you," said Violet, folding her arms.

"Why?"

"You wouldn't ask me that if you knew what they did to me and the other women."

"The countryside is teeming with the infected," said Morse. "It's not safe out there."

She held his gaze. "I don't care. Got nothing else to do. I'm not staying here."

Morse looked at Tomas. "What about you?"

"I am in your debt," said Tomas. "I help you in return."

"You're sure you know where they've taken Florence?"

"Black Heddon is all I know about," Tomas replied. "But it's better than nothing, no? I can drive the van. We have map. You can be…uh…ride shotgun, yeah?"

Morse glanced at him then Violet, grinding his teeth in his skull. "Fair enough. Sounds like a half-decent plan."

Tomas smiled. "Yes, good plan. Good."

"One thing before we go," said Violet.

Morse looked at her. "What?"

"We should bury Freya. She deserves that, at least."

\*

They dug a grave for Freya below a towering oak at the far end of the back garden. They wrapped her body in linen and lowered her into the earth. It didn't take long to shovel the loose soil back into the grave and pat the surface flat. Then they stood around the grave as the sun rose. Violet recited a poem. Once she was done and had said goodbye, they left the grave and returned to the house.

\*

Tomas packed what little food and water there was into the van while Morse gathered the men's weapons and any spare ammunition into a holdall. Violet sat Karen in a chair near the front doorway and placed a blanket over her shoulders. Karen stared at the floor.

Violet walked over to Morse. "I can use a gun."

He frowned and appraised her for a moment, then handed her a pistol in a holster with and two spare magazines. "I guess you survived this long somehow."

She attached the holster to her waist and stashed the magazines in her pocket.

"Don't make me regret this," Morse said.

She turned away and looked over her shoulder at him. "I won't."

\*

Violet helped Karen climb into the van. Tomas had laid a covering of blankets in the back so the women wouldn't have to sit on the hard floor. Once Violet and Karen were settled, Tomas shut the back doors and walked around to the cab.

Morse carried the bag of guns and climbed into the front, taking his place in the passenger seat. The map was laid on the dashboard. Tomas turned the key in the ignition and the engine started; he tapped the accelerator and listened to it growl. Then he released the handbrake and the van shot forward down the driveway.

They left the house behind.

# CHAPTER THIRTY-ONE

Morse watched the village recede in the wing mirror as Tomas negotiated between and around the wrecks of cars in the road. Violet and Karen sat in the back, huddled in blankets. No one spoke. The air smelled of sour breath and stale sweat.

Black clouds pulsed with lightning in the western sky.

The infected in the fields screamed and cried at the van as it passed them. Morse tried the radio, but there was nothing broadcasting out there. Not nearby, anyway. He thought about the outpost at Esbjerg.

The van's engine spluttered for a moment; Morse and Tomas exchanged a look. Tomas tried to hide the anxiety on his face. He gave a little smile. "It's okay, Morse. I think she make it."

Morse looked out the windscreen at the dark road and the hills beyond. "I hope so, because otherwise we're in for a long walk."

"Do not worry. My brother was mechanic and he taught me some things. I checked oil and water and tyre pressure. Everything good. If we break down, I sort it. Only problem is the roads. If they are in very bad condition, it will be hard to drive. Lucky the van is big and tough. Big wheels. Should be fine. I think will be fine."

"Fair enough. Can you drive okay with one eye?"

"Of course. I'm good driver. Only need one eye to see, anyway."

Morse checked the map and traced his finger from the road they were on all the way down the country to Black Heddon. He chewed his lip and frowned. It should be simple enough to get there, but in his experience something always went wrong. He hoped his fears were unwarranted.

They followed the signs for the A697 road and passed abandoned or burnt down houses on the way. Country roads were littered with the belongings of refugees. Makeshift graves on grass verges. He swallowed down a knot of anxiety in his throat and looked back at Violet, and she offered him a nervous smile from her place next to Karen.

Tomas guided the van around deteriorating potholes and widening cracks, and parts of the road where mud banks had collapsed and spilled onto the tarmac. Overhanging trees blocked the dim light and threw the van into shadow.

Tomas' hands tightened on the steering wheel. White knuckles. He saw Morse notice.

"I have CDs," said Tomas, wiping his mouth. "If anyone wants to listen."

Morse was about to decline when Violet shuffled forward and rested her arms on the back of the cab seats.

"What you got?" she asked.

"Not my CDs; they belonged to those motherfuckers back at the house. They used to play some of them when they took me out to scavenge for supplies. But now I took the music." He reached down beside him and produced a black CD wallet. The discs were held in polythene envelopes.

Violet snatched the wallet and went through the discs. "This one." She passed the CD to Tomas, who looked at it and made a face. "What's wrong with it?"

"Nothing," Tomas replied. "Not bad. Didn't think you like that sort of music…"

"My fiancé did. He would always play this album in the car when we went to visit my parents. Said it was the only thing that calmed him before walking into the dragons' den." She paused, took a breath. "Please play it, Tomas."

He pushed the CD into the slit in the stereo. The whirring of the stereo's insides coming to life.

Morse watched the digital display start up.

Track one.

He recognised the opening guitar chords of a song he had last heard in that long ago world before the outbreak. One among many on an album he had listened to obsessively in his younger years.

*Fight Fire with Fire*, the first track on Metallica's *Ride the Lightning* album, filled the speakers.

Morse only realised he was slightly nodding his head to the music when Tomas looked at him and smirked. He'd been remembering when he was seventeen and listening to this in his bedroom.

He stopped immediately. His foot was still tapping as he turned back to Violet. "Your fiancé had good taste in music."

"I never used to think that, at the time," she replied.

Morse faced the front and stared out the windscreen. He couldn't remember the last time he'd heard music, and it saddened him.

\*

They had to stop at some places along the narrow roads to get out and push derelict vehicles out of the way. Morse and Violet cleared the roads while Tomas kept watch. Karen was little more than a frail figment wrapped in her blankets.

They passed a house where the roof had been ripped away and debris covered the garden. Spindly shapes moved past the glassless windows. Something glistening and tentacle-like was rotting in a puddle.

Further on, Tomas had to brake hard when a pack of feral cats crossed the road ahead of the van. Mangy, thin creatures. Before they vanished into undergrowth Morse noticed the collars still in place around their scrawny necks.

"I keep thinking about all the pets," said Violet.

"I had a pet cat," Tomas said. "Someone ran it over and left it by the side of the road. By the time I found, the maggots were already inside it. Some teenagers laughed at me as I walked away with my cat in a bin bag. I loved that cat."

"I'm sorry, Tomas," Violet said.

"It's okay," he said. "Doesn't matter now."

"Shall we go?" said Morse.

Tomas put the van in gear. They kept going down the road.

\*

They drove through a cloudburst which lasted no longer than three minutes. The wipers struggled to keep the windscreen clear, even on their top setting, as the violent rain fell upon the earth. Tomas slowed the van to a crawl. Water poured from the ditches and ran off the fields. The road became a shallow river of standing water, bursting from the under the van's wheels and spraying the hedgerows.

They drove for a mile before the water receded from the road and left the tarmac wet and glistening. The branches of trees dripping into the dark thickets. A sky becoming black, consuming a drenched world.

# CHAPTER THIRTY-TWO

Two hundred yards down the road, something large, pale and spiderlike lunged from amongst a group of crashed cars as the van was passing.

Tomas shouted something incomprehensible and twisted the wheel. Violet screamed. Morse was thrown forwards as Tomas hit the brakes, and he put his hand against the dashboard to stop his inertia. His seatbelt cut into him and left him gasping.

Scream of metal and tyres, and the van veered towards the side of the road and crashed head-on into an abandoned ice cream truck. Jolt of impact. The engine cut out.

"What the fuck was that?" Tomas shouted.

In Morse's side mirror the pale spider-thing tottered into view twenty yards behind the van and almost the same size. The human faces within its pallid skin opened and closed their mouths in agonised silence. He turned to Tomas, who was fiddling with keys in the ignition. "Start the engine. It's coming."

Violet had scrambled to the back window of the van and looked out. "Holy shit." She turned back to them. "Hurry up, Tomas!"

Morse glanced in the mirror again as the spider thing crept forward then burst into a quick, loping skitter towards the van. He grabbed the MP5 and flicked the safety off. He put one hand on the electric window switch.

The spider-thing was almost upon them when the engine started and Tomas threw the van into reverse and it shot backwards. Morse watched the spider-thing increase in size in the wing mirror. Its maw opened to let out an ear-splitting shriek, as spindly limbs as sharp as knives propelled its glistening segmented body along the ground.

Morse braced himself. In the back, Violet held Karen tight to her. Tomas was completely silent and pale, staring over his shoulder to see through the van's back window.

The sickening thump and shudder of collision as the spider-thing crashed into the back of them. Heavy impact as metal hit flesh. The scrape of the creature's claw-tipped limbs along the side of the van filled the interior, and it slammed against the back doors. The van shook as if it were coming apart. The creature shrieked again and Morse covered his ears. Violet screamed but she couldn't be heard.

Tomas straightened the van and pointed down the road. Then he put it in first gear, slammed his foot down and the van shot forward. The sound of the creature's limbs upon the roof were the last thing to be heard before they left it behind.

Morse looked in the wing mirror and saw the spiderlike monster return to its hiding place amongst the cars, waiting for the next traveller.

Violet's voice was low and trembling, and barely heard above the roar of the over-revved engine. "What was that thing?"

"An ambush predator," Morse said. "Something different."

Tomas just looked across at him, his eyes wide and still terrified. He shook his head as if he couldn't believe what he had seen.

*

They turned onto the A1 as the light began leaving the sky. Tomas switched the headlights on to reveal the desolate road ahead. The dark was falling all about them. Glimpses of figures in the roadside wrecks.

The duel carriageway stretched into the distance, into nothing, chased by the headlights. Morse watched the darkness outside the window, reciting an old nursery rhyme inside his head to ignore the stiffening of his legs. He imagined what the road had looked like on the day of the outbreak and the days following. The chaos and terror. The refugees trying to leave the cities, fleeing south or north, oblivious that it didn't make any difference because the plague was everywhere.

The van slowed to weave through a place in the road where an army truck had crashed into a limo. The van scraped barely through. In the failing light he saw bones scattered around the back of the army truck and he wondered if an infected creature would make its nest in such a place.

The engine spluttered and the headlights faded for a second.

"We might have a problem," Tomas said.

"What's wrong?"

"Something wrong with engine. I think something damaged when the monster attacked us."

The van began to shudder and rattle. And when it stalled fifty yards down the road and rolled to a stop, they looked at each other and said nothing, until Violet rose from the back with a blanket over her shoulders and asked them what was wrong.

Morse stared down the road, beyond the light. "We could be in trouble."

# CHAPTER THIRTY-THREE

Tomas popped the bonnet and climbed down onto the road, glancing around the carriageway as he walked to the back of the van. Morse stepped outside and switched on the MP5's torchlight, then pulled out the retractable stock and held it against his shoulder as he swept the darkness. He followed Tomas, who was gathering a toolbox and some road flares. Morse was given a handful of lightsticks.

"You think you can fix it?" Morse said.

Tomas's face was severe and bloodless. "Have to find out what's wrong with it first. Then I fix. Hopefully. You need to keep watch."

He nodded. "Will do. Just get it fixed."

Tomas walked to the front of the van, hefting the heavy toolbox, a Maglite torch in his other hand.

Violet appeared from inside. "I can help."

He looked at her then stared out at the dark. His eyes fooled him into seeing shapes that weren't there. He blinked and ran one hand over his face. The van was surrounded by numerous scattered vehicle wrecks in the dark, negating a clear field of fire. It was decent cover for an attack. He bit the inside of his mouth as he considered it all. Trash drifted on the breeze, and there was a distinct smell of rust and decay in the air. A graveyard for the vehicles of an old world.

He felt a quiver of dread in his stomach.

"Okay," he said. "But you do exactly as I tell you, understand?"

"I understand."

"Good. Let's go."

\*

Morse told Violet to keep watch while Tomas tried to fix the van. He checked that Karen was safely ensconced in the back of the van then closed the doors to shut her inside.

He stood and watched the dark in the cold silence. He swept the wrecks with the light, and did not dwell on the skeletons strapped into their seats. Especially the ones he imagined turning their heads towards him once the light had moved past.

\*

The voice of a child came from the far side of the carriageway, past the dark shapes of dead vehicles, faint like an echo of a memory.

*"Help me…"*

Morse raised his gun towards the voice. The torchlight revealed nothing but the rusting hulks he'd been watching for the last hour. A gust of wind moved past him down the road, and he thought he heard the voice again. He looked towards the front of the van, where Violet stood watch, scanning the road ahead with her torch. Tomas grunted and clinked under the raised bonnet.

*"Help me. Help me please…"*

Morse looked in on Karen and found her asleep.

Violet appeared and shone her torch at him. "What's wrong?"

"I thought I heard something," Morse said.

"Heard what?"

"A child's voice."

"From where?"

"From the other side of the carriageway, I think. I just checked on Karen to see if it was her."

"Was it Karen?"

"No. I don't think it was."

They walked around the van, back to where Morse had been standing when he'd first heard the voice.

"Listen," Morse whispered.

They listened, motionless

*"Please help…"*

"I heard it," Violet said. "It does sound like a child."

"Out there in the dark," Morse said. The inside of his stomach was cold.

Violet aimed her torch past the crash barrier. "I don't think it's a child. Doesn't sound right."

"It's not," Morse said.

"So what is it?"

He didn't answer.

Violet took a sharp breath and raised her pistol at a point within the wrecks. "There's something between the cars, peering over the bonnet. It's just crouching there, watching us."

Morse followed her torch beam and caught a glimpse of a shockingly thin figure that darted out of sight. "I saw it."

"I saw its eyes," Violet said. "Staring right at me. Christ."

*"Please help me. Please…"*

"Oh shit," Violet whispered.

Morse looked at her. "Go to Tomas. Watch his back. Tell him to get his arse in gear."

As Violet walked to the front of the van, Morse aimed his gun towards the direction of the voice. Wrecked cars, with overgrown thickets and fields beyond. He swallowed, muttered under his breath, and blinked cold sweat from his eyes. And from twenty or so yards behind the van, from the direction they'd travelled, yet another voice drifted out of the dark.

*"Help me. Help me..."*

He checked his gun and clicked the safety off. Steadied his breathing and watched the dark. There was movement beyond the reach of his light. Thin shapes capering between the ruined cars.

And then there were several voices, all of them strangely flat and monotone.

*"Please help..."*
*"Help me..."*
*"Please help..."*
*"Need help..."*

His heart was in his throat. He looked around the vehicle wrecks, catching glimpses of gaunt faces and gleaming eyes between the cars and through shattered windows, peering over heaps of twisted metal and scrap.

He placed his finger on the trigger. "Come on, you fuckers. Let's get it over and done with."

The sounds of hands banging on sheet metal out there. Slapping footfalls on the road. He gritted his teeth and looked down the barrel. "Come on, come on. What're you waiting for?"

The report of Violet's pistol startled him. She was shouting.

He hurried towards her. When he fell in beside her, she turned around and her face was bone white and frightened.

"I've almost finished," Tomas said, without looking up from the engine. "What the fuck is going on?"

"We've got company," Morse said.

"Infected?"

"I think so. Something like that."

"I will hurry."

Morse looked at Violet. She was breathing hard. Smell of gunpowder.

"One came at me from between those two cars." She pointed directly ahead and took a breath. "I think I scared it away. You should have seen the bastard...."

"It's like they're testing the perimeter."

"The infected don't do things like that, do they?"

"I'm not sure what they're capable of."

"That's encouraging."

"Stay here," Morse said. He returned to the back of the van and looked out towards the forms of metal and glass and rust. The steel skeletons. He saw a face emerge from the dark and then withdraw again. There were wet, insect-like sounds, like bone limbs rubbing together. A vague skittering followed.

A smell came to him from his left: ammonia and old vomit.

*"Help me..."*

The voice was only a few yards away.

Morse turned and put the gun to his shoulder.

A thin shape rose from behind a car no more than ten yards away. And when the flashlight revealed its face, Morse tried to scream, but his throat closed up, and the thing clambered over the car towards him.

# CHAPTER THIRTY-FOUR

The creature reached for Morse with dripping black talons, as he fired and the white-hot rounds found the thing's chest. It collapsed five yards from him, writhing violently on the tarmac.

*"Help me…"* Words scraped from inhuman vocal chords. Its mouth didn't move. A terribly emaciated thing, with pale white skin tinged with jaundice and mottled with weeping sores. Prominent ribs and pelvic girdle. At the end of each limb, a hooked claw gleamed wetly. Hairless save for a fine wisp of downy strands on its back, its face was deathly pale and gaunt, and the stinking round maw of its mouth was lined with circumoral teeth, like that of a lamprey.

"Ugly bastard," Morse said.

The creature snapped its mouth at the air and tried to crawl towards him on its failing limbs. Morse stepped forward and put one round in its head and it fell back against the car. The last sound from its mouth was a wheezed sigh.

Out in the dark, figures scurried and darted. Morse struck the top of a road flare and threw it out amongst the dead vehicles. A gathering of thin, hunched forms scattered from the fierce red light, clicking in their throats as they skittered away.

Morse turned towards the front of the van when Violet fired several shots from her pistol. He looked back towards the burning flare, and in the light cast by it shadows were slowly encroaching towards him. Morse raised the gun and fired. Some of the infected shrank away and melted into the wrecks. He fired again; a three round burst took down a leering figure loping towards him from behind the warped bonnet of a Royal Mail van.

More of the infected emerged again, and he picked his shots and the rounds found their targets. Horrible shrieks and squeals. Violet had stopped firing. Morse hoped she knew how to reload the pistol before one of the creatures reached her.

He heard Tomas's voice, panicked and terrified.

A creature bounded towards Morse on all fours, hissing from a slack mouth. When he shot it in the face, the back of its skull burst open and black fluid splattered the ground behind it.

The flare had burnt down; the infected were gathering again. He fired another burst into the dark and rushed towards Tomas and Violet. She was reloading the pistol. There was a dead creature nearby, slumped on the road, its chest caved in by multiple gunshots. She nodded at Morse.

Tomas raised his face from the engine, oil smudged on his forehead. "Almost there."

Morse looked towards the infected and the torchlight revealed them watching from behind the cars before they ducked out of sight. "If they surround us, we're fucked."

"Okay, done," Tomas said. "I need someone to try the ignition."

Morse looked at Violet. "You do it; I'll keep watch."

She climbed into the driver's seat and turned the key. A choking sound. A rattle. The exhaust struggling through a coughing fit. Violet stopped and banged her hand on the steering wheel.

"Try again," Tomas said, his voice strained and nervous.

More choke and rattle.

"Again."

The engine spluttered and finally rose into a growl, then fell silent as it gave out.

"Almost there!" Tomas said. "One more time!"

Violet turned the key again. Something clicked inside the engine and it started.

Tomas shut the bonnet. "Give it some revs!"

Violet switched the headlights on and they revealed a languid, horribly thin figure crouching on the roof of a car five yards behind Tomas.

Violet shouted to him. The engine cut out again. Tomas must have heard the scrape of the creature's nails on metal, because he turned around and followed the shape of his own shadow to the crouching thing. He made a low sound, like a word was stuck in his throat. A screwdriver dangled from his hand.

"Get down, Tomas!" Before Morse could raise his gun the creature drew its head back and the wattle of hanging skin at its throat began to flutter and swell, and when it jolted its head forward with a sound like wet muscle ripping, it opened its mouth and a spray of pale fluid flew at Tomas's face.

Then he was screaming with his hands to his face.

An acrid stink filled the air. Hiss of something dissolving.

Morse fired at the creature and the rounds blew the frail bones from its thin chest and it tumbled out of sight.

Violet shrieked when she saw Tomas. Morse moved towards him but stopped when Tomas lowered his trembling hands. Most of the flesh on his face had been eaten away and his eyes were bleeding and sightless. The gauze patch had dissolved. His nose was gone, reduced to raw muscle. The red hole of his mouth within his red skull yawned open and the pain and terror in his excruciating, agonised scream nearly stopped Morse's heart. The palms of his hands were blistered and weeping. He muttered something in Polish and then pleaded for help, his voice pitiful and boyish, and stumbled blindly against the van and collapsed shaking on the ground.

Morse stood there, frozen with shock. Tomas held his hands out and cried. His tongue worried at his ravaged lips. His breath came in shuddering gasps and his body fell into spasm.

Morse looked down at Tomas, and was glad when his chest stopped moving, because he didn't want the poor bastard to suffer any longer.

Violet was crying inside the cab, her head in her hands. Morse shouted at her, and she tried the engine again, but there was only a dry death rattle.

Morse pulled her from the seat. "We have to go." He fired a quick burst towards the advancing creatures and covered Violet as she hurried to the back of the van. She glanced back at Tomas and her face was full of confusion and grief.

"Get Karen," Morse said. "I'll hold them off.

Violet opened the back doors. Morse pivoted just as an infected with raised claws and gleaming eyes climbed upon a car and prepared to spit. He shot the thing in the throat and its neck exploded, throwing the acid-like fluid from beneath the ruptured skin of its wattle-sac, showering the immediate area. Morse backed away and reloaded the MP5 before he downed two more infected rushing towards him. He turned back to Violet. She looked at him.

"Karen's not responding," said Violet. "She won't move. I tried to pull her out, but she's dead weight."

Morse looked into the van. Karen was just sat in her blankets, her head bowed. She was staring at the floor.

"Karen! Karen, can you hear me?"

Karen didn't move.

Morse glanced away to see the creatures moving towards them, darting between and over the vehicle wrecks. There was only one ragged row of cars between them and the infected things.

He looked at Karen, then at Violet. "Leave her."

"What?"

"If we stay, we die. She's already dead."

"I won't leave her," said Violet.

"Then you can both die together. She was doomed the moment the men brought her to that house."

"We can't leave her, Morse."

"Do you want to die? Or do you want to take revenge on the men who abused you?"

Violet stared at him, her eyes full of anger. But when Morse grabbed the bag of guns and fled into the adjacent field, she followed and didn't look back and left Karen behind as the creatures swarmed over the road.

# CHAPTER THIRTY-FIVE

They spent the remaining dark hours hiding in a tool shed in the back garden of a half-collapsed house. Neither of them spoke.

At first light Morse went outside and checked the area then told Violet to follow, and she emerged into the cold morning shivering within her clothes. She turned towards the rising sun, closed her eyes and slowly inhaled.

"Let's go back and see if we can salvage anything," Morse said.

Violet opened her eyes. "Will the spitters be gone?"

"If they've finished eating, yes."

"Okay."

They started back towards the road.

\*

By the time Morse and Violet returned to the van, the infected creatures were gone, but the stench of bile and ammonia lingered, and the bodies of those Morse had killed remained where they'd fallen. He stepped around dark bloodstains in the road. Violet walked between the cars, looking at the strewn remains around her feet.

They found what was left of Tomas. His arms and legs were flayed and scattered. His intestines had been pulled from his torso and dragged along the tarmac around the van. Most of his soft organs had been consumed. A red wound of rendered flesh and flaps of skin where his genitals had been. His skull had been broken open and the brain taken. His heart was missing.

When Morse checked the back of the van he found the insides covered in blood and everything slashed and ripped apart. Torn strands of hair from Karen's scalp on the floor. Sopping blankets stinking with fluids. All of the supplies contaminated or ruined.

Morse turned around. Violet was gone.

He found her standing away from the van with her back to him. She was staring at a trail of drying blood and gore leading away from them across the opposite lanes and into the grass and the trees beyond.

"She's gone," Morse said.

Violet wiped her face. "I know."

"She chose to stay."

"She didn't choose anything."

"We should leave."

"I have to do something."

She climbed over the crash barrier and faced him.

"What are you doing?" Morse said.

"Give me a torch and some ammo."

"You're going after the creatures?"

She took the last of the spare magazines from him. "I think they're nocturnal. Like vampires. So they sleep during the day. I'm going to find their nest."

"That's pure conjecture. They might not be nocturnal or have a nest."

"I'll find them."

"You won't come back."

Violet said, "I chose to leave Karen behind, to save myself. I'm struggling with that, at the moment, considering what she went through at the house. She suffered just like I did; *more* than I did, I suspect, and it destroyed her. I should have pulled her from the back of the van and taken her with us when we fled. So I have to do this. I don't care if it's insane. I'm sick of letting the monsters win."

Morse handed over a torch and the last road flare from his pocket.

"Thank you," she said.

"Kill as many as you can."

She nodded, slipping the spare magazines into her pockets. "I'll see you in Black Heddon, Morse."

"Good hunting."

She turned and walked away. He watched her leave.

# CHAPTER THIRTY-SIX

He was alone again. He drank some water from his canteen and then tried the van's engine, but it wouldn't start and in the end he gave up and climbed from the driver's seat and gathered his things and started down the road towards where the carriageway curved to the west and disappeared behind the trees. His legs ached with prickling stabs, and the thought of struggling down the road filled him with a vague misery. He feared blood and time.

The cold wind at his face and the first drops of rain on his shoulders. Everything utterly silent. He raised one hand and turned it over before his face, ignoring the tremor in his flesh.

A mile on, he thought he heard distant gunshots from the direction Violet had travelled.

*

He ate a cereal bar as he walked, watching the roadsides and the way ahead. It was the last of the food, and the remaining water in his canteen would only last for the day and not much of the next.

The number of abandoned or crashed vehicles dwindled until the carriageway was empty and he was the only vessel upon it. The air, so cold and aggressive against his exposed skin, went at him with little teeth.

In the road ahead, several deer picked through the mulch of dead leaves and scatterings. When he neared, they fled into the cover of thickets to his right. He felt their eyes watching him as he moved on, and he was sorry for disturbing them.

\*

He muttered Florence's name so he wouldn't forget it. Several times he saw the Burned Man watching him from the fields.

Further on he hid behind a car when he saw an infected boy crouching by the roadside, gnawing at the last scraps of dried flesh on the human skull in his hands. Morse watched for a while and let the boy eat, then stood and walked out into the road, and when the boy looked up with his stained mouth and his eyes livid with feral light, the blade of the machete made his death quick and without trouble.

Morse carried on.

He remembered the loaded marches he'd done with a full kit on his back while some arsehole sergeant-major shouted and swore at him. He never thought he'd miss those times, but he did now, and it made his heart wince. He recalled all of the good mates he'd made during basic training. Men who were like brothers. All of that seemed like another life, lived by someone else in a storybook or a frail dream.

Kicking stones from his path, he followed the carriageway to a fly-over where the corpses of a man and woman hung from the bridge railings, rotating in the breeze, their faces drawn-inwards and dried up, the skin of their bodies torn and bulging with the festering insides. Must have been dead for months. The clothes had been stripped away, even their shoes. Morse wondered what they had done, or if they had done anything, to deserve a hanging from a lonely bridge.

He saw that they both wore wedding rings, and he moved on, careful not to look back.

\*

He'd been walking for hours under the occasional glimpse of the white sun. Brief spells of soft rain. The distant calls of the infected away in the countryside. Rustling in the roadsides, a stoat scrambled through sticks and dirt, carrying a dead mouse in its jaws. It glanced at Morse before fleeing with its prey.

Every now and then, there were bones on the road. Human and animal. And next to the wreck of a smashed car, something that could have been a shrivelled, blackened heart taken from the chest of a man. He didn't stop to examine it.

The road stretched away, unending.

"This is a terrible place," he whispered.

\*

Along the road, he thought of his parents and speculated about their fate during the outbreak. They could be just bones now. It didn't take a leap of logic to surmise they were dead or infected. They were gone, either way.

He wondered if they had been living in the same semi-detached house when the outbreak hit. The house they'd occupied since before Morse was born. And he thought that if Florence was dead and he survived the next few days, he'd go to the house where he grew up, and find out what happened to them.

He halted in the road. Among a group of abandoned vehicles was a crashed hearse with all its doors hanging open. Nearby, laid flat over the inside lane, was a coffin, which he approached, irrationally worried that something would emerge – a rotted ghoul or revenant – and attack him. It was covered in grit and dead leaves, and the hinges were ruined by rust.

He stood over the casket, reaching down and about to open it, when he drew back at the last moment as his hand was upon the lid.

\*

Later, a man wearing rags and a crown made of little bones and feathers emerged from the roadside trees across the other side of the carriageway and stumbled towards Morse with his hands raised as if in exultation. Morse kept walking and raised his gun. The man traipsed across the road and stopped at the crash barrier, grinning. Saliva gleamed on his lips. His eyes shone with madness.

Morse watched him and kept a safe distance. Glanced at the man's hands for weapons, but there were none.

"None of this is real!" the man cried, the manic grin never leaving his face. "None of it! It's merely our perception of reality! It's all a dream of a memory of a nightmare, my friend!"

Morse ignored him and walked away.

"God's wrath!" the man bellowed. "Wormwood! The Jesus-Man will never return because we have rejected him! Listen to me! Please listen!"

The man's voice faded into the wind as Morse left him behind.

# THE LAST SOLDIER

\*

All of the day spent on the road. He passed the great scar of the Shotton Surface Mine. A burnt down restaurant was so much dismantled and blackened rubble. As the dim sun fell away from the earth, the sky cleared, and he knew it would be a cold night. He tried to quell his gnawing hunger with sips from the canteen, but it did little, and his need for food clouded his mind past the point of distraction.

With the darkness closing in, he left the road and started down a dirt track that he hoped would lead to shelter. He walked for almost twenty minutes, past a derelict farm where something wailed in pain, until he emerged into an open stretch of overgrown grassland. He stopped, looked around, pursing his mouth. Beyond the grassland was a long, low-roofed building with dark windows. When he saw no movement or muddled shapes in the grass he started across the field towards it.

# CHAPTER THIRTY-SEVEN

It had been a nursing home for the elderly, before the end of the world.

After climbing over the fence separating the field and the property Morse skirted around the side of the building and arrived in a gravel parking area where three rusting cars with flat tyres slumped alongside one another. They were empty, and the doors were locked when he tried them.

He turned towards the building, observing its dull façade. A flight of stone steps and a wheelchair ramp led to a set of double doors flanked either side by a small window. A languid mass of ivy and pale vines filled one section of wall from the ground to the roof. The building appeared untouched by the epidemic. No smashed glass or splintered doors. No sign of a barricade, or forced entry by the infected.

Morse aimed the gun at the front doors as he moved up the steps. A quick glance back at the waning day. The doors were unlocked and he pushed them open and edged slowly over the threshold, the carpet threadbare from the passage of visitors, residents and staff in the long ago.

He clicked the torchlight on and stood in the foyer. The dwindling daylight behind him forced the suggestion of bland walls. Faint smell of shoe polish. A noticeboard of leaflets and flyers for events and fundraisers that were never held.

He opened the door to the manager's office and stepped inside, prepared for some bleeding horror to be hunched on the floor or twitching in the corner. A relieved sigh left his mouth when nothing emerged to greet him. Above the desk, a window looked out at the side of the building, where a mound of bin bags had festered for over two years.

The filing cabinet's drawers were left open; some of the plastic folders of documents from inside were discarded on the floor. A corkboard pinned with notices and reminders, important dates and a list of minor repairs to be done by the caretaker. A watercolour painting of a meadow by an unknown artist. He wished he were there, away from the madness of his reality.

Morse inspected the desk while he kept one eye on the door he'd used to enter. He was tempted to sit in the chair and rest for five minutes, but he ended up pushing it away from the desk before searching for food in the drawers.

A paper tray of documents. Letters received and ready to be sent. An invoice for a bulk order of toilet roll. His eyes strayed to the photo in a silver frame on the desk; a woman holding hands with a little girl. Sand beneath their feet. A bucket and spade in the girl's other hand. They both had the same colour eyes. Morse tried not to think about what had happened to them, especially the girl. He remembered the dead children in the mass graves he'd dug in the refugee centres. Those plague pits filled with cadavers. His heart crumpled when he thought of their corrupted faces and twisted bodies.

He left the office and took the door at the end of the foyer, and then he was in a dark corridor that led to another door at the far end. As he swept the walls and ceiling with the torchlight, shadows retreated like wary apparitions. He moved down the corridor, but they formed again behind him and he felt them at his back and against the nape of his neck.

He stopped at the end of the corridor and put his ear to the door, suddenly aware of the silence in the confined space. Breathing out, he slowly opened the door into the room, his ticking heartbeat too loud in his head. He raised the MP5, but its torchlight dwindled before it reached the darkness at the far end of the room. He listened for the rustle and scrape of movement, the wheeze of air past sore mouths. Took a breath then released it, took one step forwards and ran the light over the walls to his flanks and the floor.

# THE LAST SOLDIER

The darkness was stifling, like he had been lowered into damp, peaty earth to roam in tunnels and caverns until he found an escape. His legs felt stiff and twisted, older than the sum of his years, but not by much. He walked slowly, carefully, every movement deliberate.

The torchlight fell over empty chairs arranged before a wall-mounted widescreen television. A game of chess left unfinished on a mahogany table. He stepped around playing cards scattered on the floor. Everything covered in dust. The air smelled of mould and desiccation. The curtains were drawn over the windows on the right side of the room, and between them was the withered corpse of a man in a wheelchair with his back against the wall. The blanket over his legs had absorbed the fluid expunged from his body after he died. His raggedy head had slumped forward until his chin touched his hollowed chest. Shrunken and wizened to little more than an artist's composition of bones in casual clothing.

Morse swung the light away and onto three bodies under a white sheet on the floor. No blood. Their feet protruding from under the sheet, clad in old slippers. He stood there and watched the lumpen shapes, wondering if some of the infected would pretend to be a corpse in an attempt to catch prey unawares.

He was about to reach down and pull the sheet away, when a scraping sound from nearby made him pause. He handled the MP5 and swept the torchlight around the room. It was a dry scraping, like the panic of a mouse in the walls. Morse turned to the man in the wheelchair, who was still dead and slumped.

The scraping stopped. Morse swallowed. He tensed his shoulders and softly held his finger on the trigger. The sudden feeling that someone was behind him became a hot weight on the skin of his back, and he turned and gritted his teeth, ready to defend himself.

Nothing there but empty floor.

He moved the light over the walls and didn't see the crawling woman until her reaching hands were almost at his legs. Morse let out a strangled cry and swung the gun around, glimpsing her awful face in the torchlight. Her mouth bulged with tiny jagged teeth, distending her jaws; the hole past her lips was full of squirming shapes. And then her hands were upon his thighs and scratching towards his crotch when he kicked her away and stumbled backwards. His finger twitched and the gun fired into the ceiling. The flash of the gunshot revealed a bloodied housecoat hanging from the woman's spindly body. Morse lost his footing in a patch of pale fluid and fell onto his back, and as he put out one hand to brace his fall he pulled the sheet away from the corpses on the floor and revealed their putrid forms.

The woman's pale hands scraped at the carpet as she moved. Blood glistening on her chin. She gurgled in her throat, gnashing her teeth.

Morse retreated against the wall and pulled his knees to his chest. When the woman scrambled towards him, he kicked her in the face with the sole of his boot. There was the crack of small bones, and she fell away into the dark, clutching her nose and mouth, whining like an injured animal.

Morse let out a breath and scanned the floor. He could hear the woman's wheezing respiration in the darkness.

The torchlight found her crouching underneath a table, scratching at her face with jagged fingernails. Blood trickled from the mess of her nose. Her eyes centred on Morse and she did not hide from the light. Her hands came away from her sagging face and she let forth a shriek from the base of her throat and skittered towards him, teeth bared and splintered.

The MP5 bucked in Morse's arms. A three-round burst. Two bullets caught the woman in the throat, while the last round found the left side of her jaw and tore open her cheek so that the broken teeth spilled from the new hole in her face.

She fell onto her front less than two yards from Morse's feet. A last wheeze from her horrid mouth.

He stood over the body. The back of her housecoat had been torn open and the skin around and along her spine was bruised and reddened. He nudged her head with his foot, and when he was sure she was dead he turned away.

# CHAPTER THIRTY-EIGHT

Morse searched the kitchen, laundry room, staff canteen and the storeroom, finding no obvious signs of violence. Only silence in the spaces of the building. He imagined the world gone silent and dead, and it brought him some comfort. No more screaming and crying, just a quiet land of desolation. Peace on Earth, which would abide until the death of the sun.

The scuffle of his boots on linoleum. His low breathing in time with his pulse, loud in his ears. He could hear the blood leaking from his heart.

He went through the residents' rooms. The decayed body of a man curled up on the floor, next to his bed, clutching an empty medication jar. His sunken face like impressions in ancient cloth. The shrivelled skin around the mouth had receded so much that he was grinning in death.

On the walls were surrealist paintings in cheap frames. Upon a shelf, a row of paperback novels bookended by porcelain ornaments. A photo of a little boy in wellies and a raincoat, laughing as he splashed through puddles. Small mementoes his eyes could not linger upon.

Just another life snuffed out. Would the man be remembered by anyone? Were all the people who remembered him dead? Morse wondered the same about himself.

He looked out the window, where the horizon was broken by the shape of a town. Just another place of dead buildings and streets. And eventually all of it would fall to ash and bone.

\*

He searched the other residents' rooms. The ones without corpses inside them smelled of lilac or aniseed, shoe leather or cough medicine. He found some of the old people in their beds, skeletal and wasted like dried-out effigies; bundles of bones in nightdresses, pyjamas and dressing gowns. Forms that belonged in coffins safe within the earth.

\*

From the front entrance he looked out at the approaching night. Strange thunder in the distance and the haunting cries of the infected past the trees and beyond the car park. Twilight shadows lengthened and thinned, reaching towards the doorway where he stood so small and vulnerable against the darkness.

# THE LAST SOLDIER

It felt like his heart was weakening in small increments. The dusk breeze fell against his face and throat.

He stepped back, closed the doors, and went back into the building to shelter for the night.

\*

Later, he patrolled inside the building, testing the doors and checking for visitors outside. He walked to the back of the building and looked out the patio doors, standing back from the glass in case something was out there watching the windows.

A misshapen figure lurked at the far end of the lawn, where it met the trees at the edge of the garden. A glimpse of weak moonlight revealed the figure as a tall man in the torn remains of the clothes he'd been wearing before he was infected. Black spines had burst through the skin of his back. He twitched and trembled, hands formed into tainted claws, staring at the sky with his mouth agape and moving in the ruin of his peeled face. Morse watched him for a long while, until he lowered his head, sniffed at the air and disappeared into the trees.

\*

Morse holed up in a storeroom stocked with boxes of cleaning agents and wholesale packs of toilet roll. Brooms, brushes and mops leaning against one corner, like they were sharing a conversation. He made a space for himself in amongst the cleaning supplies, sitting with his back to the wall and his legs crossed beneath him. The door was barricaded with boxes of bleach, washing up liquid and fabric softener.

He lit a candle he'd found in a drawer and emptied the weapons from the holdall onto the floor in front of him. Then he drank water while he appraised his meagre arsenal: forty rounds left for the MP5; fifteen left for the Glock pistol; the machete and various knives; a sawn-off double barrel shotgun with six cartridges. Also, a spare torch and three lightsticks.

Slumped against the wall he listened to the silence of the building and felt soothed by it. In the dancing light of the candle he ate dry gravy granules from a box of Bisto he'd salvaged from under a kitchen worktop. He chewed the granules around his mouth and swallowed them with little sips of water.

Later in the night, a storm passed over the building and he fell asleep to the sound of rain falling on the roof.

\*

# THE LAST SOLDIER

In his dreams he stood in the corridor outside the residents' rooms, and the doors opened and they emerged with pale hands and eager mouths. They came to him and were grateful for his offering.

\*

Morse left the nursing home soon after dawn and started across the fields at a slow walk. A dehydration headache had been persistent all night, and even now it scraped at the walls of his skull. His chest filled with thorns.

The sky was painted in grey and pulled by high-altitude winds. The ground hardened by frost, slowly thawing as the temperature started to rise to something barely above zero.

He stopped at a small colony of sickly-pale mushrooms on the edge of a ditch, crouched to examine them, and picked one from the earth. It smelled like mildew. He wasn't sure if it was edible and he didn't want to take the chance, so he left them alone and walked on with the hands of the cold breeze pushing at his back.

\*

He passed through a village called Brenkley and searched for food and water, but the few houses that been hadn't burnt down were ransacked, and there was nothing left but trash. The village shop looked to have been demolished by an artillery shell. The front doors of the small church were blackened and the ground around it was charred and dead.

An infected man, obese and naked, stumbled through wild gardens with a dead bird in his hands. Wheezing, sniffling, breathing through a mouth flooded with fluid and saliva.

Morse contemplated using the machete, but the risk of taking on such a hulking thing was too much, so when the man lumbered towards him, stuffing the bird into a slavering mouth, Morse fired twice and the man's head snapped back and he collapsed like an overstuffed sack of meat being dropped.

As Morse walked past, the man's legs twitched, so he put another round in him, just in case.

\*

He left Brenkley through the main road and passed the coal mine outside the village, stopping once to stare at the deep pits and the derelict machinery that assumed dark shapes in the dim light of the day. The reserves of coal in the earth would be untapped forever.

# THE LAST SOLDIER

And out into the fields, passing over the ancient land, checking the map then glancing around to make sure he wasn't being followed.

He walked for most of the day, skirting the northern edge of Berwick Hill and carrying on through the fields, past the village of Milbourne further on. On the way he searched abandoned farmhouses and found a tin of leek soup hidden behind an old cooker. He sat at the kitchen table in the silence of the house and guzzled the soup in minutes, cold and straight from the can. And when it was finished he wiped his mouth, stood and left the farmhouse and carried on towards Black Heddon.

In the western sky, he glimpsed a shadow in the clouds, a leviathan waking.

\*

He whispered a song from his childhood, to distract himself from the grind of his frail heart, but in the end the sound of his voice only seemed to define the pain and he walked on in silence.

\*

The sky pulsed in time to his heartbeat and his eyes were watering from the hands tightening around his heart. He ground his teeth to the point where they scraped like shale. Bunched his hands into fists and held them to his chest, digging his fingernails into his palms. He looked around, his vision framed in dull flashes. There was nothing out here but him, the road and the silent land as he gulped for breath.

Then he looked ahead and stopped, and his hands fell away to his sides. His mouth fell open.

The Burned Man waited for him at the crossroads.

He wiped his eyes then pulled at his face with stiffened fingers. Maybe this was his death-dream and the road which he walked would lead straight to hell.

*

The Burned Man beckoned him with one hand. *Come closer. Do not be afraid.*

Morse approached the crossroads, stumbling upon the cracked tarmac like a blind beggar, muttering incoherent thoughts. When he reached the crossroads he stood before the Burned Man and said nothing, staring into his face. And the Burned Man grinned at him with the whitest teeth then raised his hands to Morse's head and caressed his hair. Morse started crying. The Burned Man lowered one hand until it was over his chest and then dug his fingers into Morse's flesh to reach for his heart.

# CHAPTER THIRTY-NINE

Morse woke sweating and hyperventilating from his trance-state with his hands scratching at his chest and a frantic cry in his throat. He looked down the road to where it entered the woods, and in the trees he saw several hooded figures watching him, motionless between the thin dark trunks. Their faces were hidden, and they clutched rifles to their bodies.

They moved towards him silently through the trees.

Morse raised his gun stepped to the side of the road, to hide behind the protruding foliage, but as he crouched he heard the crunch of feet upon stones behind him and before he could turn around the tip of a barrel was put to the back of his head, and all he could do was raise his hands and hope the bullet would take him cleanly.

*

The armed men came down the road and stood watching, with their rifles aimed at him. Others emerged from behind Morse and surrounded him, their faces obscured by gas masks or flaps of cloth with eye holes and torn slashes for their mouths. They wore poorly-fitting combat fatigues under their dark jackets. Heavy boots moving silently over the ground.

They were dressed like the men in the whorehouse, and those who abducted Florence. A cold hand gripped his spine.

The Order of the Pestilence.

The barrel of the gun was taken from the back of his skull. One of the men snatched his MP5 from his hand while another took his other guns and then patted him down until he was relieved of every weapon and piece of ammunition.

Cold sweat beaded on his forehead. His tongue stuck to his palate. Lips dried to paper. One of the men, a tall specimen with broadly sloping shoulders, put a gloved hand to Morse's face and tilted his head, examining his neck, looking for bites, puncture wounds and signs of infection. He stretched Morse's eyes wide to scrutinize them. Morse didn't resist, even when the man shone a halogen penlight into his eyes to leave a blurred afterglow on his vision.

The men were silent.

The tall man stepped away but still faced Morse. There was a Glock pistol in a quick-release chest holster on his tactical vest. An SA80A2 rifle hanging from one shoulder over his long, thick coat. The black portals of his eyes in the gas mask were apathetic towards him.

The men took hold of Morse and tied his hands behind his back. Then they pulled him towards the trees, and he was sure he would die.

\*

They took him through the woods and onto another road where a military truck waited. They threw Morse into the back of the truck and most of their number climbed in after him to sit on the benches either side of the vehicle. Two of the men lifted him up and seated him, and he did not look into their faces or attempt to struggle. The canvas canopy obscured the outside world. The men were but shadows around him.

The engine started with the heavy growl of some carnivorous animal. The truck trembled around him. The men were muttering, but he couldn't discern what they were saying. And when the truck started down the road, rattling and bouncing over and around potholes, Morse bowed his head to his chest and wondered who the men were and what they wanted with him.

# CHAPTER FORTY

The truck began to slow a few miles on and then idled for a moment. Morse heard men's voices and the sound of metal gates being opened. He kept his head bowed and his eyes down. The plastic binding chafed his wrists. When the truck moved on, he sensed an ending to the journey, and soon enough the truck stopped again and the men began to disembark. Two of them grabbed him by his arms and dragged him along and he jumped down to the ground with them, and he only didn't fall over because they took hold of him again. He looked at his feet. Thick grass and mud. The men didn't release his arms.

He blinked at the dim light and looked back the way the truck had come, down a dirt track towards a large metal gate set into a high stone wall that stretched a hundred yards before it vanished beyond the curve of a rise in the ground.

He was jostled away from the truck, and when he looked up in the direction they were taking him, he saw a great manor house about two hundred yards away, set against the grey sky. Around the house were canvas shelters and tents in military green. Several trucks, vans and Land Rovers were parked nearby. Figures in combat fatigues and jackets ambled around the tents and vehicles.

"What is this place?" Morse said.

The men answered by pulling a burlap sack over his head, and took him towards the house.

\*

They had taken Morse to a room, where he now waited at a metal table, his hands tied to the back of the chair he sat upon. Across the table was an empty chair. His arms were aching and stiffening. At least the men had removed the sack from his head.

He looked around the room. There was nothing on the table or the walls. Strip lighting stung his eyes. The floor was concrete. He shivered in the cold air.

All of his weapons, equipment and clothes had been taken, and they had dressed him in shabby hospital scrubs. His bare feet were filthy and his toenails needed cutting.

The door opened. Raising his face from his chest, he watched the door swing inwards and realised he was biting the inside of his mouth.

A tall man entered the room. He had a long, greying beard and his shaven scalp was painted with runic tattoos. He appraised Morse and said nothing. Morse glanced at the pistol in the man's chest holster and recognised something in the way he was standing, straight-backed and rigid. He wondered if the man was ex-army.

The man stood to one side of the doorway as an older man entered the room clutching a walking stick in one gnarled hand. He wore a thick woollen turtleneck sweater under a tweed jacket. Corduroy trousers down to black shoes. His head was completely hairless; even his eyebrows were missing. He was short and very thin.

The man looked over at Morse with a slight frown on his face. Eyes that appeared agitated around the edges, as if he were sensitive to the light. He squinted slightly as he walked to the table and sat down on one of the chairs, wincing as he bent his knees. He leaned on the walking stick with both hands resting on it between his legs. He looked at Morse.

The tall man closed the door and stood against the wall.

"Hello," the old man said. His voice was soft and well-spoken. One side of his mouth curled.

Morse shifted in his chair. "Hello."

The old man moved his fingers on the top of the walking stick. "We know who you are."

"Yeah? Who am I?"

"You are Joseph Morse."

"And who are you?"

"My name is Alec Jardine, and behind me is my dear friend Guthrie."

Morse glanced at Guthrie then looked back to the old man. "How do you know who I am?"

"I believe we have a mutual friend. A girl."

"Florence?"

"Correct."

"Is she alive?"

"Of course she's alive."

"You abducted her. You took her away from me."

"In a way, Morse, that is true. It is also true that you killed two of my men."

"Self-defence," Morse said. "They tried to kill me."

"I understand. I would have done exactly the same. I actually quite admire your tenacity. How exactly did you find us?"

"One of the men I killed had a map in his pocket."

Jardine raised his eyebrows. "You've come a long way. I commend you. Guthrie thinks you're ex-army. He saw the tattoo on your left arm. He used to be in the Paratroopers, you know. What regiment were you in, may I ask?"

Morse hesitated. "Irish Guards. A long time ago."

"See much action?"

Morse tried to push away the images of the Burned Man and the dead people in bombed out buildings. "Northern Ireland. A few other places."

"Commendable. I've always had the greatest respect for our armed forces."

"Our armed forces are gone."

Jardine touched the sagging skin under his jaw. "And that is a great shame. They fought so bravely against the infected, but it was all in vain."

Morse stared straight into Jardine's eyes. "Is Florence okay? Have you hurt her?"

Jardine looked genuinely shocked. "I would never hurt Florence; she is a very special girl, as I'm sure you know. That's why you both returned to Britain, is it not?"

"You know about her…gift?"

"Oh yes. She indeed has a gift, a very special one."

"Can I see her?" Morse asked.

"Not at the moment," Jardine replied. The overhead light glistened on his scalp. "I don't think that's wise."

"Is that her choice or your choice?"

Jardine smiled, thin and humourless. "A mutual agreement."

"If you've hurt her, I'll kill you." Morse's shoulders tensed and blood fill his head.

Jardine's smile faded. His eyes hardened. "No need for threats, Mr. Morse. You seem to misunderstand the position you're in. Florence is happy with us. She wants to be with us. We are her family now, not you. She no longer needs your protection. We are not her captors; she came to realise she is supposed to be with us. And you're alive only because she persuaded me not to execute you. This is my favour to her. You should be thankful for your life."

Morse's pulse filled his head. Worms seemed to writhe under his skin. "Where are we? Are we near Black Heddon?"

The smile returned to Jardine's hairless face. "About two miles from the village. A place called Darlington House. It used to belong to some distant relative of the Queen, and was turned into a refugee shelter during the outbreak. Eventually the refugees abandoned this place. Then we found it and made it our home."

"You're the Order of the Pestilence," Morse said.

Jardine raised his eyebrows. "You've heard of us?"

"A little bit."

"Well, news doesn't get around like it used to." Jardine paused and dabbed at his mouth with a handkerchief.

Morse sniffed. "You sound like a bunch of oddballs."

Jardine merely smiled. "We are devoted."

"Devoted to what?"

"The Plague Gods."

"Well, that's insane."

"We see the Plague Gods as kindred beings that have come to this world to spread the gospel of their flesh. They want us all to join with them."

"By becoming infected," Morse said.

Jardine shook his head. "No, not at all; the Plague Gods have promised my people the gift of ascension. It is something much more than mere infection. We will become part of them and we'll experience true joy."

"You're deluded."

"You lack faith. The Plague Gods have blessed us. This is the next step in evolution. My men are righteous."

Morse spat on the floor. "If you're all so fucking righteous, why did you have a whorehouse upcountry?"

A note of confusion in Jardine's voice. "Excuse me?"

"Your whorehouse. Where your men kept women in squalid little rooms and chained them to their beds – where your men killed them."

"It's more of a waystation for my soldiers, when they're further up north. My men need to satisfy their urges. That's just the way it is. Men need release from war. Women serve their purpose when they're on their backs."

"I killed all your men at the whorehouse," Morse said.

Jardine blinked and looked past Morse's shoulder. "I see. That's unfortunate. But let's put that to one side for now."

Guthrie didn't move, but his eyes never left Morse. Always watching.

Jardine picked at one fingernail. "You see, Morse, like Florence I have a gift. The same kind of gift; and I too have felt its pull upon me recently, beckoning me to the south, where ascension awaits us all. That was the direction you and Florence were heading when my men encountered you, right?"

"You have some sort of a connection with the Plague Gods, just like Florence?"

"Yes, in a way."

"How?"

"They came to me in my dreams. They tainted me somehow. I sensed Florence before I even saw her. I knew she was out in the wastelands, within reach; it was like a homing beacon. Florence is very gifted. She even knew that you were nearby; that's why my men went out to intercept you. All the children here are gifted."

Morse frowned. "There are other children like Florence?"

"Yes, Morse. We've been waiting for all of the children to join us, and Florence was the last one to arrive. And we will be leaving soon, but you will not be joining us."

"So you're going to execute me, after all."

Jardine wiped his damp mouth with the handkerchief, then folded it and tucked it into his jacket pocket. "I considered keeping you as a slave, but I fear you'd be too much trouble. We have something else in mind."

# CHAPTER FORTY-ONE

There had been no food or water in the hours since Morse had spoken to Jardine. The lights had been turned off, and he remained tied to the chair, staring into the pitch black, swallowing the lump in his throat as his lower body became numb.

No sounds of movement or activity outside the room; no footsteps or voices. Maybe they had left him here to rot. But Florence wouldn't let that happen, would she?

He wondered if the room was flanked by others. He tried not to think of cool fresh water in his mouth and down his throat. How long did he have left until his heart gave out?

Unknown time passed and his vision dipped in-and-out of focus. So tired. Everything fading.

When he passed out he dreamed of terrible gods with human faces.

*

He woke terrified in the darkness, breathing hard through a dust-filled mouth, cold sweat dripping from his face; his nerve endings were on fire, and he was certain someone was here to kill him. Tensing at the anticipation of an unseen hand upon his shoulder, hunched over and trembling, he tried to gather spit inside his mouth.

On the other side of the room, near the door, a small flame appeared in the dark, and beyond it was a face revealed in the flickering light. A visiting phantom.

"Florence," Morse whispered; his voice dry and painful at the back of his mouth. He was unsure of the vision facing him from across the dark. "Is that you?"

She approached on soft footsteps. The smell of the burning candle. The low scuffle of her white robes upon the floor. She stood beside him, put the candle on the table and placed a bottle of water to his mouth. Looked at him with something like pity. He drank from the bottle, hesitantly at first, but as the cold water sluiced over his teeth, gums and tongue and down his throat, he gulped several mouthfuls before Florence pulled it away. He sat there gasping. The water bloated his stomach and loosened his guts. Florence screwed the top back on the bottle. Morse was scared to look at her in case closer scrutiny revealed her as a pale figment and she'd melt away into the dark.

"It's good to see you, Morse," she said with genuine warmth in her voice. Morse's heart burst. "I was worried about you."

"I'm okay," he said. "Have they done anything to you, Florence? Anything bad?"

"Jardine has taken care of me. He has a gift too."

"Yeah, he said."

"The Plague Gods will make us into something greater than human. More evolved."

"This is insane, Florence. Untie me and I'll take you away from here."

"You have to let me go," she said.

"I can't. I promised to protect you."

"You did protect me, Morse. Your work is done."

"You're like a daughter to me, Florence."

"And you've been like my father, for all this time, since you found me. I wouldn't have survived without you. But now it's time for me to move on. Nothing can stop the ascension. Me, Jardine, the other children; we're all linked to the Plague Gods. It's why I was called back to Britain. We have to go to Hallow Hope."

"Hallow Hope?"

"It's where we'll find ascension."

"They've brainwashed you, Florence."

"They've helped me. I see colours and hear sounds you will never understand. In my dreams I speak to the Plague Gods and they tell me things you wouldn't believe. All sorts of secrets. And I can hear your fragile heart, Morse, ticking down to its eventual end. It's tired, and so are you."

"This is madness, Florence. The Order has killed people. They've killed women."

"You have to let me go, Morse. Don't come after me."

"I can't let you go."

"You have to."

"I can't…"

"Goodbye, Morse."

# CHAPTER FORTY-TWO

He sat in the dark, shivering and mumbling, reciting the names of people he'd known in the long ago years.

The Order of the Pestilence had departed for the south. When he realised he'd been left behind in the locked room to die of thirst, he was overcome by hysteria and panic, and he kicked at the table and thrashed in his chair until his legs gave way and he collapsed to the cold floor.

He lay on his side, tears on his face, nodding his head to the beat of his heart and whispering to the room's occupant ghosts.

\*

Unknown time passed. In the cold dark, the memories of old army mates came to visit him. The memory of Belfast kids throwing stones at him on his patrols. He'd been screaming for a long while, but now he was silent, and in that silence he heard their footsteps and scrabbling hands on the floor. Whispering his name. Naming his sins. Pinning the blame. When he closed his eyes, it made no difference to the dark.

His army mates gathered around him. They were muttering something, but it was muffled, as if their mouths were stuffed with cloth or their heads were bowed too close to their chests. He asked them what they wanted, but they ignored his questions and kept muttering and gibbering. They smelled of ash and blood.

He craved water and tried to remember the taste of it in his mouth. Delirium filled his mind. Waking dreams about thirst and isolation. He whispered his service number, name and rank. Prayed to pagan gods. Asked for Christ, Vishnu and all the terrible entities of mythology. But only the Devil answered and spoke warmly of preparing the way for his descent to hell.

\*

Morse was talking to his old mate Pete Simmonds, who had been killed by an IRA sniper back in 1989. Pete said how he missed fried egg and chips, and Morse laughed and didn't stop laughing until the banging at the other side of the door startled him and silenced Pete's complaints about the dripping mess that had once been the back of his head.

The banging wasn't real. He was merely disorientated by the thirst in his throat and the ravaging hunger in his gut.

"Who's there?" His voice was a mere croak. He licked his scabbed lips, but there was no moisture on his tongue to dampen them. "Who's there? Is that you, Florence? Have you come back to help me?" His throat was raw, filled with brambles and sand. His limbs felt petrified.

The sound of bolts being pulled back. The click of the lock echoed inside his head. His eyes widened as the door opened and a small light appeared in the doorway and swept towards him. He cowered from the light, like a distressed child.

The torchlight found him, stinging his eyes. The breath rattled from his chest. "Florence? Have you come back for me?"

A voice came to him. "I've found you."

RICH HAWKINS

# PART THREE

# ASCENSION

# THE LAST SOLDIER

# CHAPTER FORTY-THREE

Florence wandered the shores of the fjord in the dark, listening to the lap of the water and the distant cries of sea birds. She looked at the sky and the pitch black of it made her feel small and terribly lonely. She wrapped the blanket tighter around her shoulders and kicked at small stones by her feet. She stared at the dark water for a long time, trying to summon the will to walk into the shallows and then the deeper depths, because that would mean the end of all suffering and pain, and she could join her loved ones. The infected would never have her if she took her own life.

She kept going along the shore.

The great shapes of the mountains beyond the fjord tempted her, and she remembered all those people who had gone up there to die. Florence thought she might do the same, but she was too tired and scared to leave the shelter of the encampment, and she'd probably collapse before she reached the mountains.

She turned around and headed back to the camp.

*

# THE LAST SOLDIER

*Her torchlight meandered over canvas walls and flaps as she wandered amongst the tents and makeshift shelters. The silence filled her head. The abandoned belongings of refugees scattered like trash. Opened suitcases and clothes, empty food packaging and small mounds of used batteries. Fish bones in a cold campfire. Smell of ashes and piss on the breeze.*

*She stood in a small clearing within the camp and looked past the gathered tents, out to where the water led to the sea. She thought of home and all she'd left behind. She thought of her school friends and her teachers, her cousins and her uncles and aunties. Her mum and dad. They were all gone. What would they say to her now?*

*A sound in the sky directly above her, like whale-song from a much greater creature. A cry from cavernous lungs and chambers. She looked up. In the pitch black clouds, she sensed rather than saw something, and she knew it saw her, too, and it regarded her with the appraisal of a human to bacteria. Then there was a great pressure upon her, grinding on her bones. A feeling of insects swarming inside her head and scraping their little limbs over her brain. Her nose was bleeding and she could taste the blood as it dripped into her open mouth.*

*She fell to her knees and tried to turn away from the sky, but she couldn't look away because the thing bearing down on her would not allow it, so she opened her mouth and screamed and then collapsed onto the cold stones and dirt.*

*The last thing she saw before she fell into the dark was the silhouette of the great sky-thing backlit by strobe-flashes of pale lightning. And then the sky filled with thunder and there was nothing else.*

\*

*A light was shone into her eyes as she woke shivering and crying. A figure in a gas mask stood over her. There was a rifle slung over his shoulder and a pistol in his belt. He smelled of engine oil and smoke. She looked up at him, at the black eye holes of the gas mask, and stifled her cries with her hand over her mouth.*

*Behind the man, other people in similar masks surveyed the encampment, sweeping their torches over the abandoned tents and scattered rubbish.*

*"Please," she said to the man. "Please help me."*

*The man took hold of her and helped her to sit up. He gave her his water canteen and she drank deeply until she was gasping and coughing.*

*She flinched when he pulled his mask off because she was scared he'd have a monster's face instead of a man's.*

*He smiled at her. His sad eyes. "Are you okay?"*

*She drank more water as she nodded.*

*"What's your name?"*

*She wiped her mouth. "Florence."*

*"Nice name."*

*"What's your name?"*

*"Morse. Pleased to meet you, Florence."*

# CHAPTER FORTY-FOUR

They had been on the road for two days; it had been four days since Violet rescued Morse from Darlington House. He was weak and stumbling like a drunk, holding his arms to himself in the cold. Violet helped him stand straight when he faltered. The rain murmured as it fell. They needed food and water. They were exhausted and freezing.

"Have to keep heading south," Morse said, his voice muffled within the hood of the coat Violet had found for him in the previous house. The trousers she'd scavenged were too short for him and stopped just above his ankles.

Violet said nothing. She watched the fields, looking for the infected, and the road for signs that the Order of the Pestilence had passed through here in their vehicles.

"Hallow Hope," Morse said. "Hallow Hope."

\*

They arrived at the high ground outside a village, cowering from the rain. The downpour shrouded the black hills.

"We need food," Violet said, her head bowed away from the sky. "We have to go down there and see if we can find something."

Morse nodded, slow and listless; his face crumpled by melancholy. The despair and exhaustion in his eyes forced Violet to turn away. Something had happened to him in the darkness in that locked room. He had lost something about himself. She once had a friend who'd lost her baby son to meningitis, and was never the same afterwards; even when she'd smiled it was humourless and cold. The last Violet saw of her was only a few days before the outbreak hit. Morse reminded her of that friend.

Violet checked the pistol. Only three bullets left. She checked the knife in her belt.

Morse stared at the village down the hill. Red-rimmed eyes, bloodshot and squinting. He looked broken and wrecked, bedraggled and forlorn. Violet pitied him, but she would take care of him because he had saved her life before and she didn't want to be alone out in the wasteland of Great Britain.

\*

The rain soaked them long before they entered the village. They walked the main road, past streetlights, derelict cars and dilapidated houses. Violet entered the grocery shop while Morse waited outside frowning at the shattered windows and the post box which had been broken into and emptied.

Violet searched the shop and its backrooms but there was nothing, and when she returned outside the disappointment on her face must have been obvious because Morse turned away and stared down the road to where two cars had collided on the vicarage lawn.

They went through the houses, watching for infected or other survivors. Violet searched a row of bungalows and found all the cupboards looted bare. She thought their luck was out, until she stumbled upon a stash of bottled water and tins under some loose floorboards in a house whose scarred, stained walls told of extreme violence committed long ago. She couldn't believe her eyes; but she reached out and touched the supplies and lifted them from their hiding place and knelt staring at them until the crazed smile left her face. She kissed one of the water bottles and muttered her gratitude to whoever had left the stash there. Maybe they had been killed before using the supplies or had simply forgotten and moved on. She opened one of the bottles and drank. When she was finished, the bottle was half-empty. She wiped her mouth and exhaled deeply. Her thoughts seemed a little clearer now.

Violet was almost on the verge of tears as she looked at the tins, anticipating the taste of mandarin segments in syrup. Then she went back out into the street with the supplies in two string bags she'd found in a cupboard. Morse looked at her then the supplies and gave a wan smile that broke her heart.

Violet gave him one of the bags. Morse nodded faintly. His shabby trainers scuffed on the road. There was a distant look in his eyes as he held the bag to his stomach. Violet knew he was thinking of Florence.

\*

Violet found a house without corpses, bones, or the leavings of wild animals inside. They shut the doors and blocked them with furniture, then closed the curtains.

She lit their only candle, recovered from the trouser pocket of a corpse she'd stumbled upon in a field before finding Darlington House. Examining the food tins for punctures, she listed them to Morse, who stood the bottles of water by the wall. Vegetable chilli, meatballs in tomato sauce, sweetcorn, new potatoes, haricot beans, mandarin segments, peach slices, pineapple chunks, and three tins of fruit cocktail.

"Which one do you want?" Violet asked him.

He regarded the gathering of tins, one hand at his mouth. "Peach slices, please."

She handed him the tin, watched him pull back the ring and sniff at the contents. He pinched a slice of fruit between his fingers and lifted it to his mouth, bit into it and chewed. He closed his eyes and swallowed. Then he bowed his head and put one hand to his face, and Violet realised he was weeping.

\*

Violet ate the tin of mandarin segments then drank the remaining syrup in one go. Her heartbeat quickened and her skin tingled. It was wonderful. She hadn't eaten mandarin segments since well before the outbreak. She licked juice from her lips and fingers then slumped back against the wall.

Morse watched her while he sipped water.

"You okay, Morse?"

He took the bottle from his mouth. "I can't believe you're alive."

"I could say the same to you."

"When we parted back at the van, I was certain you'd die."

"Thanks for your confidence."

"Did you destroy the nest?"

"I killed them all."

"Impressive."

"Their nest was in an old building site. They were asleep when I found them, curled around each other. There were bones and scraps of clothing on the ground. I found Karen's head."

"How did you kill them?" Morse asked.

"There was a litre bottle of turpentine in a tool shed. Poured it over them as they slept, then I chucked in the road flare you gave me and the bastards went up in flames. Even then some of them tried to attack me, so I shot them. The ones I set on fire took a while to die."

She could still smell the turpentine on her hands and hear the screams of the infected creatures as they burned and reached out to her.

"What did you do afterwards?"

"I walked. When I arrived at Black Heddon it was deserted. Then I saw the Order's soldiers going back and forth from the manor house. So I watched and waited, hoping to see if you were there, until they all left in a convoy of vehicles and headed south. I found you in that room on the basement level. In the dark."

Morse's face tightened, like he was recalling a bad memory.

Violet said, "You told me that the Order wanted ascension. What does that mean?"

Morse snorted. "Nothing good. Something about the next stage of evolution."

"They think being infected is the next step in evolution?"

"Somewhere in-between, I think."

"That's fucked up."

"The worst thing," Morse said in a low voice, "was when I spoke to Florence, she seemed like a different person, like she was someone else. Brainwashed. I saw the look in her eyes, in the way she looked at me. It wasn't her. Not really her."

Violet was unable to look away from the pain in Morse's eyes. "I'm sorry."

Morse grabbed a blanket and pulled it up to his neck. "I'm going to get some sleep."

"Okay," she said. "Goodnight."

"Goodnight."

\*

While Morse slept, Violet walked around the rooms with her torch, studying the artefacts of the former inhabitants. Faded photos of children making silly faces. Pictures of cute dogs. Small mementoes and relics. A shelf full of ornithology books and porcelain doves. A sideboard crammed into a corner, topped with a platoon of plastic toy soldiers.

She went through a white door into the garage attached to the side of the house, and stood in the dark, sweeping the torchlight over a dull green Land Rover Defender. The painted metal gleamed under a layer of dust.

She whistled lowly. "Well, hello."

Apart from the deflated tyres, the vehicle was in good condition. She found a set of keys on a wall-hook in the kitchen and climbed into the vehicle. When she tried the ignition there was nothing but a dry clicking. She tried again and it was the same. Then she tried once more and then gave up because she was worried the sound would attract any nearby infected.

After she'd popped the bonnet, she checked the battery then the water and the oil. She stood there and inhaled. The smell of cold engines brought back memories of helping her dad fix his car when she was a little girl.

# CHAPTER FORTY-FIVE

In the morning she left Morse in the house and went out into the desolate village. She didn't know its name, and didn't care.

The sky was dark grey, but without rain. Her trainers scraped over the road and shards of shattered glass. She watched the houses for movement. Crows squabbled over the dead body of one of their own, bedraggled and crumpled in the road. A fox appeared in the road ahead of her and darted away when she approached.

The mechanic's garage was at the outskirts of the village. It was a small, independent garage – probably family-owned before the outbreak. A metal sign swung from a chain on a post. **Chant, Bradshaw and Park's Motors**. Not exactly catchy.

On the forecourt were rusting, bird shit-splattered cars with price-signs stuck to the inside of their windscreens. Weeds prospered around the wheels.

The front of the building was a small office with intact windows. She opened the door and stepped inside the reception, stepping past faux-leather seats once used by customers while they waited for their cars to be brought around the front. A fake potted plant. The beige wallpaper made her eyes ache.

The rot-stink hit her immediately, and she stepped back, grimacing, before she continued.

A drinks machine was trashed. She rooted around in the remains, but all the cans had been taken. In the office at the back a dead man slumped over his desk; skeletal and rotting in his shirt and tie. A scalp of wispy hair above a face which was no more than a blackened skull whose remaining scraps of flesh were like putrid jelly. One of the countless dead.

Violet found a packet of cigarettes and a lighter in the pocket of the man's suit jacket hung over the back of his chair. A full pack. She pulled one out and sparked up next to the dead man, then sat on the edge of the desk and smoked slowly with hands shaking from the sudden burst of nicotine.

She allowed herself a small smile and knew she'd have to ration the cigarettes in future.

\*

As rain began to fall she went out to the garage at the back of the property, and aimed her pistol and torch into the dark mouth of the entrance where the large sliding doors were open just enough for someone her size to fit through. She stood and waited for something to rush out at her, but when nothing emerged she stepped inside and tried not to panic at the swarm of the dark about her. She moved the torchlight over the inside of the garage, across the floor and up-and-down the walls, breathing silently. The smells of engine oil and WD-40 were like bittersweet memories.

She swept the torch over hydraulic presses and racks of tyres, stacked tool boxes and jacking beams. Diagnostic machines, engine cranes, and emission analysers. While she searched amongst the various equipment racks and stands, looking for a battery compatible with the Land Rover, she scavenged a lump hammer and a crowbar, and put both of them into an empty gym bag she'd found under a workbench. In a tool chest, she uncovered a packet of cheese and onion crisps beneath some gloves.

Eventually she found the correct battery and put it in the bag. Struggling to lift the bag, she slung the strap over her shoulder and emerged from the garage, into the dull light of the day. The rain had dwindled to drizzle. There was thunder far away.

An infected man in overalls staggered from the birch trees on the other side of the property; he was wretched and hunched, almost skeletal, and he halted and sniffed at the air. When his gaze fell upon Violet, tendrils emerged through the torn holes in his overalls and swayed in the air, dripping pale fluid from their sharp tips. His face contorted into a snarl and his mouth slowly split open down the middle to display an inner maw of serrated teeth.

The creature charged towards Violet. She dropped the bag, put away the torch then raised the pistol, took aim and bit down hard on her lip. The taste of smoke in her mouth. The rise and fall of her heart. She fired and the bullet took the man through his right thigh, and he fell forward. His hands clawed at the air, and he tried to rise, but before he could climb onto one leg Violet put the pistol away, took the lump hammer from the bag and walked over with the intention of breaking his body into pieces.

## CHAPTER FORTY-SIX

Morse was slumped on the sofa when she returned to the house. She gave him the packet of crisps she'd found, which he ate while she unpacked the crowbar and lump hammer from the gym bag. They looked at each other and said nothing. Morse finished the crisps and screwed the packet up then dropped it behind the sofa.

\*

In the vague light of the garage Violet fitted the battery while Morse held the torch beside her. It took her a while to remove and replace the old battery, and when it was done she tried the ignition and after four attempts the engine started with a muffled crack of the exhaust. She revved the accelerator and then let the engine tick over. According to the fuel gauge there was just over half a tank left. She hoped the diesel hadn't deteriorated too much.

Morse opened the garage door to disperse the smoke and watched the street while Violet used a foot pump to inflate the tyres. Afterwards, her legs ached and throbbed, and her face was slick with sweat.

She turned towards the doorway. Morse looked back at her.

"I think we're ready to go," she said.

\*

Violet smoked and drove while Morse navigated from the seat beside her, surveying a road map he'd found in the glove compartment. The roads outside the village were mostly clear of car wrecks and obstructions. Rain pattered against the windscreen between the screeching of the wipers. The tyres ground upon the deteriorating tarmac and kicked up puddles and grit.

They passed the dark stain of Newcastle away to the east. The countryside faded to dull tones. Infected people wandered the land, wailing towards the sky in the pouring rain; abject creatures slumped and impassive as if in mourning for the dead world. Morse watched them and could only feel pity for their distressed lethargy. A man clad in soaking rags, kneeling in the mud, reached one hand towards them as they passed, his face broken with pain and misery.

They made slow progress along the country roads and had to turn back at the dual carriageway when it was blocked with traffic jams of derelict cars. A

Waitrose lorry was jack-knifed over a flyover. Infected dwelled among the dead vehicles, lurking like tired transients.

There were infected on the back roads too, hunched over next to vehicle wrecks or crawling from ditches with a look of idiot hunger on their faces. A woman in an Avenged Sevenfold t-shirt, with wiry tendrils spilling from her skin-tight face, stumbled into the road and the Land Rover clipped her and she tumbled away with arms flailing.

They passed a pile of gathered shopping trolleys by the roadside, left there like the last example of modern art.

The things they saw watching them from the fields and amongst the trees. Violet kept her foot down on the accelerator.

Occasionally Morse had to get out and clear the road of fallen branches and the left behind possessions of refugees who were now long-dead and gone from the world. Personal effects and paraphernalia. He opened a luggage case and rifled through the clothes inside; took a woollen hat, two scarves and a large-sized jumper. When he stared at a photo album opened at a page of sunny beach snapshots, Violet had to press the horn to wake him from his reverie and warn of writhing figures emerging from the trees behind them.

He climbed back into the vehicle and gave one of the scarves to Violet.

\*

When some roads were impassable, Violet took the Land Rover across fields and scrubland. The rough ground shook the vehicle and jolted them in their seats. Violet drove carefully to avoid a puncture.

After they returned to the road, they passed an infected girl of no more than six years old with a sodden teddy bear still in her hand. Morse had to look away from her sorrowful face. He turned to Violet; she looked at him then turned to face the road again. She had seen the girl too. There was nothing to be said.

\*

The roads the Order had taken on their way to Hallow Hope were cleared of obstructions and wreckage.

They had covered fifty miles by the time the light faded from the sky. Violet stopped the car next to a field. There were fresh tyre tracks in the roadside mud. In the field a man had been tied to a wooden cruciform and his heart cut from his body and burnt in a small campfire nearby.

Morse and Violet stood looking at the dead man. His head was bowed to his chest. Neither of them wanted to look at his face. The red hole in his chest glistened. A sliver of white bone was visible.

"Looks like a sacrifice," Morse said.

Violet prodded at the cold ashes with her foot. "Didn't the Mayans rip out the hearts of sacrificial victims?"

"That was the Aztecs."

"Yeah, them as well."

"Old rites," Morse muttered.

Violet looked at the dead man. "What was he sacrificed to?"

"The Plague Gods."

"Sick fuckers."

Morse stared across the fields. "Blood sacrifice."

\*

Morse swapped with Violet and drove for a while as darkness fell about them and covered the land. He turned the headlights on. Violet found a Johnny Cash CD and listened to *The Man comes Around* over and over again until Morse had a headache and switched it off despite her protests.

They stopped and left the engine running while they drank water and ate. They kept the doors locked.

Morse stepped outside and pissed in the grass. Then he got back inside, put the vehicle back into gear and started down the road again.

\*

They travelled parallel to a railway for a few miles. An abandoned train left upon the tracks. Four carriages burnt out from the insides and no glass in the windows. Charred metal. The suggestion of skeletal forms in some seats. Morse slowed as he passed the train and thought he saw a lone spindly figure walking along the aisle in the last carriage, and he was sure it turned to look at them as they went past.

\*

They emerged onto the A1 motorway and passed Sunderland within the hour. Violet was asleep. Morse kept the speed below sixty, mindful of abandoned cars and trucks in the dark. The clattering of his pulse as he worried about Florence and what was happening to her. The guilt and shame of failing her. The fear that she was beyond his reach and he couldn't help her. It was like a hole in his heart, aching with remorse.

# THE LAST SOLDIER

He glanced at Violet sleeping, her face barely distinct in the dark. He hoped she was dreaming of good memories.

# CHAPTER FORTY-SEVEN

*A Sunday morning. The sun rising above the treetops. Violet and Ethan held hands along the pathway running through the nature reserve and past the dark serpentine river. They talked and laughed and tried to remember what happened the night before at her uncle's 50$^{th}$ birthday party in the function room of a three-star hotel.*

"You were so drunk," Ethan said. He was tall and dark-haired. His shoulders were thin, but she was fine with that; her last boyfriend was obsessed with going to the gym and looked like a fitness model, but he ended up being an arsehole. Ethan was completely different. He didn't drink protein shakes three times a day, pluck his eyebrows with tweezers, or take longer than her to get ready for a night out.

"I was not drunk," Violet said.

"Liar."

"You were drunker than me."

"Ah, so you admit you were drunk then..."

She looked at him, tried not to smile. "A little bit. You're a lightweight anyway."

"Don't change the subject."

"I'm not. It's not my fault you can't handle your ginger beer."

"Ginger beer? Piss off."

*She laughed. He playfully punched her shoulder.*

*"That hurt."*

*"Quit whining, woman."*

*"Cheeky twat."*

*"Yeah, I know I am. That's why you find me so irresistible."*

*"You wish."*

*"Oh, come on, I am one sexy mother."*

*"Are you still drunk?"*

*Ethan laughed. "Maybe a little bit. I blame your dad for making us do those tequila shots at the bar."*

*Violet felt her stomach churn at the memory. "Yeah, they were nasty."*

*"I can still taste them."*

*The pathway opened out into a meadow. They followed a trampled track through the grass and climbed a fence and stopped by the river. She noticed that Ethan's face was quite sweaty and clammy. Probably the alcohol. He'd just recovered from a nasty cold, and had made the most of it by getting her to be his servant for two days, bringing him soup and buttered toast whilst he stayed in bed watching episodes of* Buffy the Vampire Slayer *and* The Office *while drinking Lucozade.*

*Ethan looked at her then quickly looked away, wiping his mouth and sniffling.*

*"Are you okay?" she asked him.*

*"Yeah," he answered too fast. "I'm fine."*

*"Are you sure?"*

*He nodded. "Yeah, yeah. Definitely."*

*"You're acting weird."*

*"I'm fine."*

*They walked on, watching squirrels dart along tree branches and crows circle in the sky.*

*Then Ethan stopped. He faced her. His expression was serious, and that worried her a little. A muscle twitched under his eye and his mouth opened a little to show his teeth. He brushed a strand of hair away from his face.*

He's going to break up with me, *she thought.* Three years, all for nothing. It was his flat, so I would have to move out. *All of these thoughts went through her mind.*

*She frowned. "What's wrong?"*

*"We need to talk, Violet."*

*He knelt upon one knee and looked up at her, one hand in his jacket pocket. And he pulled something from his pocket. A little box coated in velvet, which he opened, and inside was a ring so delicate and beautiful she was speechless.*

*Ethan swallowed, bit his lip. "Violet Harrigan, will you marry me?"*

*Violet felt her legs weaken and her stomach turn upside down. She looked from Ethan to the ring then to Ethan again. She opened her mouth to speak, but there were no words. She felt lightheaded.*

*"Violet…?"*

*"Uh…"*

*"Are you okay?"*

*Her face broke into a wide smile. "Of course I'll marry you!"*

*Relief swept over Ethan's face. He took the ring from the little box and placed it over her finger. The ring caught the light like it was magic. Ethan stood and they hugged and kissed. Then they hugged again. He wiped the tears from Violet's eyes.*

*The ring was a perfect fit as Ethan slipped it over her finger.*

*"I love you," she said, looking up at him.*

*"Back at you," he said, smiling. "I've got to say, that's a fucking relief."*

*She grinned, examining the ring, turning it in the air so it sparkled. "I thought you were about to break up with me."*

*"That's stupid."*

*"You're stupid."*

*"We'll be stupid together."*

*"Okay."*

*They walked on, after more hugs and kisses.*

*Violet couldn't wait to tell her family and friends. She was tempted to text her best and oldest friend Sandra, and tell her. Although she hoped Sandra wouldn't be jealous, seeing as she had just broken up with her boyfriend. She tried to imagine her mother's face when she told her. She hoped Dad would be okay with it; he had always told her never to get married too young. But she was twenty-three now, an adult, and she knew what she was doing. Ethan was the man for her, even with his horrendous flatulence after eating pizza.*

*She put her arms around him as they walked. He stroked her hand and said it would be a beautiful day.*

*"It is already," Violet replied.*

*Ethan pointed across the field, to where a man had emerged from the trees. She looked towards the man and squinted. He was about fifty yards away, stumbling through the grass. Part of his t-shirt was ripped. He was jerking his head around, like there was a wasp buzzing around his face. Violet thought his face was twitching, but she couldn't be sure because of the distance.*

*He was heading towards them.*

*"What's wrong with him?" Violet said.*

*"Maybe he's got a hangover too."*

*"Can we turn back? I don't like the look of him."*

*He smiled at her. "I'll protect you, my wife-to-be."*

*"Oh, my dashing hero."*

*"That's right, baby."*

*They turned around and started walking back up the river. Violet glanced back and saw that the man was following them. He did not look away from them and had shortened the distance to less than forty yards. His mouth was moving. Violet thought she could hear him gibbering. She thought there was blood on his hands. It could have been red paint. Yeah, red paint…had to be.*

*"Walk quicker," she said to Ethan.*

*He glanced over his shoulder and frowned. "What the hell…?"*

*They quickened their pace.*

*Violet checked behind to see the man had gained on them, and now he was only twenty yards away and loping into a staggering run. Perhaps he was only out for a morning jog…*

## THE LAST SOLDIER

*With red paint on his hands and a torn t-shirt...*

*He was almost upon them when Violet screamed.*

*Ethan turned around and raised his hands as the man lunged forward and took hold of him. And before he could protest or even ask what he was doing, the man jerked his head towards Ethan's face and seized the skin of his cheek in his mouth. Ethan screamed, his eyes going wide with shock and pain. Violet couldn't move. The man pulled his head back and tore away a patch of skin from Ethan's face. A sound like ripping cloth. Blood spurted and covered his lips and chin. Ethan pawed uselessly at the man, who knocked him to the ground and fell upon him, snapping jaws working against the torn mess of his face and throat. Ethan screamed wordlessly. Called out to Violet. His legs kicked at the air.*

*"Leave him alone!" Violet screamed.*

*The man raised his face from Ethan's trembling body and stared at her, his mouth hanging open and bloodied. Bits of Ethan were on his face and down the front of his ripped t-shirt.*

*Violet bunched her hands into fists as she backed away. She risked a glance at Ethan; he wasn't moving. His eyes were open and staring at the sky. His throat had been opened and most of the skin was gone from his face. Violet was muttering, crying, and wiping her eyes, trying to stand upright, because if she collapsed now she would suffer the same fate as her fiancé.*

*"Oh god," she whispered, close to hysteria. "Oh god, help me." She said Ethan's name as she realised he was dead. Her lovely, poor, sweet Ethan, gone. Gone. Dead. There would be no*

*engagement party and no wedding, no marriage and no children. No life together. Nothing. She felt reality falling away and she wondered, absurdly, what her mother would say when she got home.*

*The man rose from Ethan's lifeless form and started towards her, reaching with bloodied hands.*

*She turned and ran.*

\*

*Violet fled up the pathway and into the stretch of woodland that would take her back to the street directly outside the nature reserve. She cried and wailed as she ran, senseless and beyond logic. There was thunder in the sky, and she thought that was strange because there had been no clouds only a short while ago.*

*The man bolted from the trees to her right and bundled into her. They fell down together. She landed next to him and rolled away just as he swept out a hand that raked across the ground. She shuffled backwards, using her hands to move. He crawled after her, snarling, his eyes wild and bloodshot.*

*She backed up against the bottom of a tree trunk and the man bounded forwards like a crazed animal. She drew her foot back and kicked him in the face. He flinched, but it barely slowed him down and then he was upon her, his mouth opening wide. She noticed how sharp his teeth were. The teeth that killed Ethan.*

*There was a large stone in her hand.*

*She swung the stone at his face and connected with his left eye, and he fell away shrieking. She rose into a crouch and when he recovered and came forward again, she hit him on the side of the head and he collapsed stunned to the ground. A horrid wheezing drifted from his mouth as she knelt over him on one knee.*

*"Who the fuck are you?" she said, at the edge of madness. "Why did you kill my Ethan? What's wrong with you? Why? WHAT'S THE MATTER WITH YOU?"*

*The man growled in his throat as she brought the stone down again and again until his face was caved-in and destroyed, and all recognisable features were nothing more than red pulp. Then she sat and threw the stone away and cried for a long while under the canopy of trees, staring at the blood on her hands. Grief and terror blanked all rational thought and there was only the savage cry of murder in her head. Shadows danced around, limbs as thin as the tree branches above her. Black dots imposed upon her sight. Voices and sirens on nearby streets. A child crying. Dogs barking. The thunder was louder.*

*It sounded like the world was ending*

\*

Violet woke with tears in her eyes. She looked at where the engagement ring had been on her finger, and couldn't remember the last time she'd seen it.

She thought about Ethan and wondered if he was waiting for her in some other place, with his family and her family, and all their pets. All of those who'd died in the outbreak.

She would never forget them.

# CHAPTER FORTY-EIGHT

They stopped in a layby. Morse slumped in the passenger seat as Violet took her turn to drive. He was exhausted. His eyes struggled to stay open. He yawned into his hand and looked out the windscreen at the shapeless dark.

"Where are we?" Violet said as she clipped in the seatbelt.

Morse blew air from his mouth and rubbed his face as he checked the map. "A few miles north of Nottingham, on the M1."

"We've still got to go around Birmingham?" said Violet.

"Yeah."

"We haven't got much fuel left. I don't know how far it'll take us."

"Let's just keep going."

Violet put the Land Rover in gear. "Fair enough."

\*

Morse tried to sleep, but his hands were jittery. He sipped water and downed an aspirin. Every time he started nodding off, he jolted awake with a breathless gasp. Violet asked him if he was okay. He nodded, said nothing, and then stared into the dark at the fleeting glimpses of roadside ruins.

\*

A few miles on they found a boy in the road, scratching at his face and mouth with his fingernails. Violet stopped the Land Rover. The scrape of the tyres on loose gravel. The boy stood there in the headlights, side-on to them, and when he turned towards the vehicle his eyes gleamed and the blood on his face was brighter than any red Morse had seen before.

Morse leaned forward, staring through the windscreen. "It's one of Jardine's children. He's wearing the same kind of gown as Florence."

Violet gripped the steering wheel. The engine idled. "Do you think he's dangerous?"

Morse already had his hand on the door release. "I'm going out to talk to him. He might be able to help us." He put the pistol in his pocket and stepped outside. Apart from the sound of the engine, there was utter silence out on the motorway. Beyond the reach of the headlights, the darkness swelled and thickened.

The boy turned to Morse and regarded him with watery eyes. A little boy lost. Despondent. A form barely aware of itself. His skin was puffy, reddened and irritated where his fingers had been busy. Morse couldn't imagine what it must have been like out here in the darkness, alone and wandering.

"Hello," Morse said. He kept his distance, careful not to scare the boy. Violet emerged from the vehicle and closed the door. The boy glanced at her, raking at one corner of his mouth.

Morse took one step forward. "Are you okay?"

The boy looked at him and stopped scratching. "They left me behind. Jardine left me behind."

"My name is Joseph," Morse said. "I can help you."

The boy appraised him. "No one can help me now."

"What's your name?"

The boy blinked slowly. "Daryl Duncan."

"Pleased to meet you, Daryl."

The boy nodded at Violet. "Who's she?"

"I'm Violet."

"Like a flower."

She snorted. "Yeah, that's right."

"Tell me what happened, Daryl," Morse said.

"The thing inside my head; that connects me to the Plague Gods. Something wrong with it. Something wrong with me. Not working properly. Malfunctioning. Jardine said I wasn't special anymore and of no more use; that I wasn't worthy of ascension.

He told me I had to be discarded. I just wasn't feeling very well, that's all. I had a bad belly. And I've been looking forward to the ascension since Jardine found me. Now he's abandoned me. What did I do wrong?"

Morse stepped towards the boy. "You've done nothing wrong, Daryl."

"I feel bad."

"You don't need to feel bad. None of this is your fault."

"No, I feel ill again. My belly hurts." He placed his hands on his stomach. And before Morse could go to him, the boy hunched over and vomited blood and bile onto the road around his feet, retching horribly as the muscles in his neck stretched tight.

Morse stepped back. The boy fell to his knees as more fluid spilled from his mouth. He was making an awful sound, like he was being strangled. His bulging eyes flicked towards Morse and the pain in them was severe.

"Get back here, Morse," Violet said.

Daryl collapsed writhing onto his side, clutching his stomach, whimpering and mewling. Bloody vomit covered his garments and the lower half of his face.

"Morse." Violet's voice was shrill. "Get away from him!"

Morse didn't move.

"Move! He's turning!"

The boy turned onto his back and arched his spine and his mouth opened in a silent cry. His hands scraped at the road. His legs kicked. Something tore, and Morse realised it was the boy's clothes as sharp, insectoid limbs and appendages erupted from his stomach and chest. His human limbs fell still and hung limp. He was gasping. Such pain and terror in his eyes. A tortured scream rose from his mouth as his body was ravaged and transformed. His face began to fold inwards like melting plastic. Violet put her hands to her mouth and stared, unable to move.

Morse could watch no longer. He took the pistol from his pocket and walked over to Daryl, standing out of reach of the jerking insect limbs. He raised the pistol and fired two rounds into the vulva-like maw of the boy's face. And then Daryl stopped moving and his glistening pale limbs slowly trembled and faltered until they went still. They remained upright, curved towards the sky.

Morse turned and looked at Violet. She climbed back into the Land Rover and sat in the driver's seat, staring at her lap, her face deathly pale and slack. Morse returned to the vehicle and sat beside her. They said nothing. The silent dark seemed to thicken beyond the windows.

They left the boy on the road and carried on.

\*

Morse had fallen asleep thinking of the boy and the monster he would have become. When he woke and smelled smoke in the air, he swivelled towards Violet and saw she had a lit cigarette in her mouth. She drove carefully, scanning the road ahead.

"You okay, Morse?"

He clenched and unclenched his hands, staring at his knuckles as they whitened each time. "I feel useless. I couldn't save Florence from the Order, and I couldn't save that little boy."

"You did save that boy," Violet said. "You put him out of his misery. Better to be dead than infected, or whatever he was becoming."

"What if we reach Hallow Hope too late and the ascension has already taken place? What then?"

"I don't know, Morse."

"Will Florence transform like the boy did?"

Violet tapped the end of her cigarette into the ashtray. "The boy said there was something wrong with him. Malfunctioning, didn't he say? Fuck knows what that all means. Maybe Florence isn't malfunctioning. I don't know how this shit works."

"I don't know if I could shoot Florence, if she transformed."

"If it was to put her out of her misery, you would, Morse. I know you would."

He looked out the windscreen. The motorway stretching away from them into the mist. "Maybe. I don't know."

Violet took one last drag on the cigarette then put it out. "Get some more sleep, Morse. I'll drive from now on. I don't want to sleep anymore. I've no wish to dream again."

# CHAPTER FORTY-NINE

Past Birmingham and Coventry, Warwick and Stratford-upon-Avon. They travelled the M5 towards Cheltenham, and stared in silent awe at the town's destruction. Past the Cotswolds, which were beautiful even in the harsh and unforgiving grind of winter. There were no infected on the roads as the sky brightened in the east and the darkness began to recede.

Morse glimpsed in the wing mirror and saw movement. A black dot slowly growing larger behind them. He rubbed his eyes then looked again. Something far back on the road, gaining on the Land Rover.

He turned in his seat and looked back down the road.

"What's wrong?" Violet said.

"We've got company."

Violet looked in the rear-view mirror and muttered something under her breath.

The SUV weaved between crashed cars over the damp road, closing in on them. Its bumper was fitted with a snow plough, which it used to shunt wreckage aside as it screamed down the road. When it closed to within thirty yards, Morse saw hooded men in cloth masks seated within.

"It's the Order of the Pestilence," Morse said. He grabbed the pistol and looked at Violet. "Drive faster."

She put her foot down and the engine whined in response.

\*

The SUV rammed the back of the Land Rover and jolted it forward. Violet struggled for control of the steering wheel as the Land rover juddered and rattled. Morse gripped the sides of his seat with bone-white fingers. Violet glimpsed in the rear-view mirror, her face screwed into in a panicked, wide-mouthed frown. She kept her foot down on the accelerator, the Land Rover darting between vehicle wrecks, kicking up scraps of rubbish and debris.

Morse looked back at the SUV as it closed in and again hit the Land Rover's back end. Screech of metal crumpling. Hard impact. Shattered plastic. He was thrown forward until his seatbelt cut into his chest.

There was a metallic rustling from the rear of the vehicle, like something coming loose. Violet swerved to avoid the stranded cars on the road, but could do nothing when an infected man covered in cysts and blackening lesions lurched from behind the derelict hulk of an ambulance. The Land Rover hit him just as he swivelled towards it and opened his ravenous face, and he burst like a sack of rotten meat across the road. Blood and shreds of flesh covered the windscreen. Violet turned the wipers on, smearing the blood over the glass, until she put them on full speed and the windscreen only cleared several yards from the back end of a crashed lorry.

Violet wrenched the wheel at the last moment and the Land Rover swerved across the road, the tyres shrieking.

Morse breathed a burst of hysterical laughter and shook his head in disbelief.

The SUV kept pace with them and then closed in again, trying to get level the Land Rover now that the road was clear of most obstructions.

Morse glanced back at the SUV and checked the pistol.

Violet kept her foot down.

The SUV was now just behind and to the side of the Land Rover, no more than five yards between the vehicles. Morse swallowed, breathing deeply, biting his lip, his hand tight on the pistol grip.

When he looked back at the SUV a man emerged from the sun roof, clutching a double-barrelled shotgun. His face and head shrouded by the cloth mask and hood. He levelled the shotgun at the Land Rover.

"Oh shit," Morse muttered. He buried his face against his chest and put his hands over the back of his head. Violet screamed and turned away.

The gunshot shattered the windows over the back passenger seats. A surge of cold air. Tiny glass granules were scattered. Violet cried out.

When Morse looked up again, the SUV sideswiped the Land Rover and pushed it across the road. Grind and scream of metal. Stink of engine oil, exhausts and smoke. Burnt rubber and chemicals. The Land Rover's tyres fought for traction on the damp road, and this time Violet lost control and the vehicle lurched to one side and across to the opposite side of the motorway, through a gap where the crash barrier had been torn away by an accident during the outbreak. The tyres screamed and skidded, and the Land Rover veered from the road and down a grassed slope, shuddering and rattling like it was falling apart, then into a barren field. Violet clenched iron fingers around the steering wheel; sweat dripped down her face, her skin bloodless and clammy, and her eyes bulging wide. Murky water and mud sprayed from under the wheels. Clumps of dirt dislodged and flew in all directions.

Morse's heart was palpitating as he looked back and saw the SUV come down the slope and into the field.

"Keep going," he said to Violet. "They're following. They're not giving up."

Violet was muttering under her breath. Morse thought she was praying.

*

They emerged onto a narrow road. Morse glanced back, but didn't see the SUV behind them.

Violet said, "If the road's blocked at some point, we're fucked."

"I know. Keep going."

She slowed the Land Rover to skirt around a rusting Volvo crashed halfway into the hedgerow. Half a mile further on, they entered a village. Violet kept at a steady speed through the deserted high street. Morse glimpsed movement in some windows and gardens; staggering figures reacting to the sound of the engine.

There was a crossroads ahead, directly in the middle of the village. A set of traffic lights, and a church further on.

The Burned Man stood by the roadside as they passed. He stared at Morse without expression. His blackened skin wept from glistening cysts. He moved his mouth slowly, as if invoking something old and forgotten.

When the Burned Man grinned, Morse looked away.

He whispered the man's name and apologised.

"Did you say something?" asked Violet.

They were halfway through the crossroads.

Morse went to answer her.

The SUV came at them from their right and there was barely time to shout a warning before the plough on its front swiped the Land Rover from the road.

# CHAPTER FIFTY

His vision trembled and he put his hands to his face and groaned as the world shuddered in the aftermath of the crash. Violet was murmuring something as she tried to raise her head from her chest. Morse looked towards the front of the car, where steam was rising from the engine, and the bonnet was crumpled and hanging open after hitting the garden wall. The stink of engine coolant and hot metal. The airbags had already deflated.

Everything blurred, dipping in-and-out of focus until nausea swelled in his stomach. He ached all over and his head was pounding. He pawed for the seatbelt release, and when he was free he grabbed the pistol from the footwell and climbed out of the Land Rover on unsteady legs. When he took a breath it ached through his teeth. He closed his eyes to stop the ground from moving underneath him.

Looking back down the road he saw the SUV trying to reverse out of the slopping mess of a rock pond, its wheels spraying up brown water and mud.

Several infected began to emerge from ruined houses and beneath piles of debris. Filthy, shivering creatures crawling from their nests. They headed towards the SUV, hands grasping at the air, their mouths working like mechanical traps. Men, women, children. One woman slithered from underneath a mound of bones and trash and went down on her knees as tumultuous appendages and stingers burst from the dripping cavity of her torso. Her limbs twisted into sharp points and she went onto all fours and skittered in the direction of the SUV, mewling like a sickly newborn thing.

Morse pulled Violet from her seat. "Are you okay?"

She nodded and looked at the ruined front of the Land Rover. "I'll live." She leaned against the side of the Land Rover and held her leg, while Morse retrieved the bag with their meagre supplies inside.

"Let's get out of here," he said. "We seem to have agitated the villagers."

Violet took the lump hammer from her pocket. Morse slung the bag over one shoulder, the crowbar in his hand. The pistol was tucked under his belt.

They hurried down the road, away from the Land Rover, just as more infected appeared from between the houses, drawn by the sound of the SUV's engine and the gunshots.

The men of the Order were fighting off the infected. Pained shrieks and cries stirred the air. Morse glanced back to see two of the men stood either side of the SUV, firing pistols at the diseased villagers, who fell in their disordered ranks.

Violet gasped and grimaced, trailing her right leg slightly. Morse helped her along as they approached a short stone bridge flanked with iron railings.

"You should leave me here and go on by yourself," she said through gritted teeth.

"Don't be fucking stupid. Keep moving."

An infected man in a ripped chef's tunic stumbled from the doorway of a half-collapsed building, painfully contorted and gasping. The man sighted them and opened his mouth; the squirming horror of his tongue flicked at the air past his teeth. Another infected creature appeared behind him, covered in dirt and encrusted fluids, its neck swollen with rippling tumours.

"Keep moving," Morse said, trying to move faster. Violet moaned at the pain in her leg. "We're not giving up now."

*You should shoot her*, a voice at the back of his mind said. *She's slowing you down.*

He shook his head.

*Do it. Survival of the fittest. You'll die with her, otherwise...*

More infected emerged from the other side of the road, slavering and squealing.

*Shoot Violet in the leg. Cripple her. Escape. Survive.*

The infected screamed and wailed, hungry for flesh, lost in a haze of bloodlust.

*Do what you always do. Survive when others die.*

Morse pulled the pistol from his belt, swallowing the knot in his gullet. He looked at Violet. "I'm sorry."

She turned to him. "Sorry for what?"

He let out a rasping breath. He felt sick.

"You're worrying me, Morse…"

When he spoke, his voice was calm and ordered. "Go on alone, while I keep these fuckers busy. I'll catch up. I promise."

"Morse…" Confusion in her eyes.

"No argument. Just do it. I'll find you."

"But…"

"I'll see you again, Violet."

She looked at him, then grabbed either side of his head and kissed his brow. "You're a stupid bastard, Morse."

He smiled wanly and handed her the bag. "Just go."

She turned, stumbling away, and glanced back over her shoulder as Morse stood in the middle of the road and waited for the infected to reach him.

\*

Violet spied the shallow river beneath her as she hobbled across the bridge and then down the narrow street. She entered the churchyard, caught in the shadow of the church tower looming above her. Glancing around to make sure she wasn't followed, she stepped amongst the old graves, using the headstones to support her weight. She winced and stopped, then tried to continue, but in the end she slumped to the ground with her back against one of the gravestones, exhausted and sore, watching the rise and fall of her chest while she tried to regain her breath. The lump hammer's grip was slick with sweat as she held it tightly.

The gunshots from back up the street sounded so distant. She exhaled in shuddering breaths. Her eyes were stinging with tears. A wave of regret at leaving Morse behind swept through her body in juddering bursts. She hoped death came quickly for him.

It began to rain. She made a sound like the beginning of hysterical laughter, staring up at the sky with her mouth open. And stayed that way for a short while, and only when she heard the pattering of limbs nearby did she lower her face to meet the spindly-legged thing coming towards her from between the graves.

# CHAPTER FIFTY-ONE

Morse stood on the small bridge, flanked by old metal railings, and shot the first infected that reached him. The shuddering old man whose back was covered in needle-thin spines collapsed near his feet with his black heart blown from his chest.

He put the pistol away to save the last round for himself and raised the crowbar as a woman in the flapping remnants of a dressing gown reached for him with raw hands. And when the crowbar impacted with her face, it crumpled inwards and she fell down wailing until Morse silenced her with a downward swing that broke her skull and exposed the glistening pulp of her brain.

More infected came for him – disjointed and frail, murmuring in spasmodic bursts – and he killed them all, crushing their skulls and shattering their bones until their broken bodies lay around him and he was last man standing. They had been weak, malnourished creatures, like starving street addicts. He felt no pride in their murder.

After he wiped his eyes of tears he looked down the road. The SUV was facing towards him. The masked men of the Order watched from behind the windscreen. They had killed the other infected. Bodies sprawled all over the street. Gardens of flesh and twitching piles. The stink of them was abhorrent. More death in the shattered wastelands.

Morse stared at the SUV, his shoulders sagging and tense with exertion, his limbs heavy and aching.

The rev of the SUV's engine was the only sound.

Morse spat, wiped his mouth with his fingers. Nowhere to run. A flickering image of Florence appeared in his mind. He said her name and smiled through the pain of his mouth.

The masked men watched him.

He took the pistol from his belt and considered using it on himself, but it felt pointless when so many others in this damp hell wanted to take his life instead.

The SUV started towards Morse, tyres screeching and over the tarmac and building up speed until it was screaming straight for him down the road.

He raised the pistol. Took aim, steadied his hand with the other, and as he let out a ragged breath he pulled the trigger.

He said her name.

The bullet pierced the windscreen and took the driver in the chest; his hands flinched on the steering wheel and the SUV veered to the side of the road, passing Morse by less than an arm's length as it crashed through the bridge's iron railings and plunged to the river below.

Morse fell to his knees and dropped the pistol, lowering his face to the surface of the road. A burst of laughter that wasn't his own slipped from his mouth. Then he crawled to the side of the bridge and looked down to the shallow river. The SUV had landed on its roof, and two of the men were trying to climb out of the battered vehicle; flailing in the water, their masks fallen from their faces, soaked and gasping. The wheels were still spinning. Smoke rose from the underside of the vehicle.

The infected were upon the men as soon as they emerged from the SUV, tearing and biting, dragging the men onto the riverbank to pull them apart. And when they were done with them, the infected reached inside the vehicle for the other men and pulled them out through the water. One of them regained consciousness at the same moment a girl pierced the top of his head with the stinger that emerged from her gaping mouth, and he screamed until the other infected smothered his face with their own. Then there was merely the sound of meat being sucked from his skull and his legs kicking on the riverbank stones.

Morse lay on the road, staring at the sky. When the rain started falling he was grateful and hoped it would wash him clean.

*

As he was limping past the graveyard, Violet rushed out to meet him, her hair and face dusted with soil, and her eyes manic like she'd seen something from her nightmares. She fell against him, breathing hard, trembling. She looked up at him.

"It was digging them up," she said. "Scavenging on the dead."

When Morse looked towards the churchyard, he glimpsed a thin shape on gangling legs darting between the headstones, and he told Violet they should leave before it grew tired of bones ransacked from old graves.

# CHAPTER FIFTY-TWO

Four miles south-west of Bristol.

The mist had moved in less than an hour ago as they walked along the motorway. They listened for footfalls and wheezing breaths. Morse looked at his shaking hands. Violet offered him a weak, awkward smile. He faced forward, where he could only see a dozen yards down the road before it faded into the mist.

"Are you okay?" she asked.

He nodded. "Yeah. You okay?"

"I'm okay."

"You sure?"

"Yes."

"Good."

\*

The mist absorbed the ambient sounds of the land and cloaked it all in silence. They found a truck loaded with antique furniture; some of it had spilled onto the road in the long ago and now most of it was rotting and splintered. A mahogany table and a grandfather clock.

A sideboard. A piano tilted at an angle on the road, its back legs snapped and buckled.

Violet raised the fallboard and tinkled the piano keys.

"Did you play?" said Morse.

She ran one finger over the lid, lost in thought. "Not really. My mum tried to get me to learn with a private teacher when I was sixteen, but I never took to it. And the teacher was an old perv who kept trying to look down my top."

Morse spat.

The truck's cab was burnt out. Anonymous bones all blackened and covered in ash. The steering wheel was a charred relic. A roasted boot in the driver's footwell.

They walked on.

"I dream about flying," Violet said.

Morse watched the mist. "Like Superman?"

She snorted. "No; I'm in a plane. A 747…or something like that, and I'm in my seat and other passengers are in their seats. People going on holiday and honeymoons. Happy people. Families. All that shit. There're usually a few celebrities amongst us."

"Like who?"

"That bloke on that kids' show."

"Which one?"

"Doctor Who."

"Was it a kids' show?"

"Seemed to be when I watched it."

"Fair enough. Which Doctor was it?"

"The one who's Scottish, but put on a Cockney accent."

"David Tennant?"

"That's the one. He was in the Harry Potter films too."

"I didn't know that. What happened in the dream?"

Violet's face darkened. She pursed her mouth. "They all get infected, and I'm only the one that's still normal. And I can hear the screams inside their heads and they're begging me to help them. Then something happens and the fuselage bursts open and we're all pulled out and then I'm falling – we're all falling – but we never hit the ground."

"I have no fucking idea what that means," said Morse.

She laughed without humour. "Me neither. It's just dreams, isn't it?"

"Reality is just as fucked up. Has been for a while."

"Absolutely. My grandad would have called it God's Wrath."

"Really?"

"Big time. He was all about that sort of shit. What about you?"

"I don't know. I don't think it matters now…if it ever did."

"Grandad used to say 'the hearts of men are fickle and greedy'. Stuff about the 'folly of man', whatever the fuck that is. Pretty mental."

"Sounds like a people person."

"Only if you believed what he believed."

"I knew plenty of people like that."

"He was still a good man, in his own way," Violet said. "He tried his best. Died of a heart attack on Christmas Day in 1998."

"Sorry."

"It's okay."

Morse stopped.

She halted beside him. "What's wrong?"

"Listen." He frowned, squinted into the mist ahead and to the right. He could hear the sound of harsh breathing drifting towards them, like someone with a lung infection struggling for air.

Violet looked at him. "I hear it."

And when Morse turned his head to follow the sound he saw a man limping along the other side of the carriageway, partly-shrouded by the mist, thin and mangled, coughing blood onto his chin and chest. A sickly wraith in flapping clothes holding his hands to his throat while a low growl ensconced in fluid escaped from his mouth. His feet scraped over the road, and when he was gone Morse and Violet remembered to breathe again.

*

They were passing through the Mendip Hills. Through the mist, the faint forms of slopes and rises could be seen. A road sign ahead. KEEP APART 2 CHEVRONS. Morse grunted.

"Do you still want to do this?" he asked Violet. "You can leave, find somewhere safe. You could survive."

Violet scratched her face. "You're not getting rid of me that easily."

"Fair enough." He checked the map and tried to estimate their position. He thought that Banwell was to their east. The villages of Christon and Luxton were somewhere to the west.

They arrived at an old army truck abandoned on the motorway. A hulking shape with no shadow.

Violet looked up at the vehicle. "This belonged to the Order."

Morse checked the truck, but there was no one inside and no supplies left behind. He spat.

Violet walked around to the front of the truck and returned a few seconds later. "Looks like it ran out of diesel. Engine's cold."

Morse looked on the ground for any signs that Florence had been there. He only gave up when Violet said they should move on, and he agreed and followed her down the road.

# CHAPTER FIFTY-THREE

As they went on, Morse stared at the TrafficMaster cameras atop four metre tall poles. Sensors and antennae. All of it dead. No one was watching.

A cluster of buildings to the left of the motorway past a wire fence. Possibly a factory. A sign for a metalworks.

They kept walking, their feet dragging on the road. Crackle of grit. Stepping over weeds, rags and trash. Dead leaves. The top layer of tarmac was crumbling in places.

"The mist smells of decay," Violet said.

"I imagine most of the world smells like it," Morse replied.

Much further down the road, they came to a road sign.

## WELCOME TO SOMERSET

"You've come a long way, baby." Violet spat a laugh out.

Away to the left, in a shrouded field, the thin shape of an electricity pylon emerged like an abandoned wicker man. A dead sentinel on the Somerset Levels.

\*

They'd walked for hours, and now the dark was closing in and all about was the dying of the light.

"We should get off the road," said Violet.

They cut across a wild field and entered a hamlet of several houses where nothing moved or made any sound and the buildings welcomed them with open doors. They moved slowly, carefully, listening to the mist and watching its tendrils close around their legs then dispersing again when they moved.

Violet led them to a house on the very edge of the hamlet and stepped through the doorway, sweeping the insides with her torch. She knocked on the jamb and waited. Morse gripped his crowbar and looked around, and when he turned back to Violet she nodded at him and moved further inside the house. He followed, closing the front door behind him.

Violet waited for him in the hallway.

Together they searched the house for infected.

\*

They sat around two birthday candles fastened to a nub of Blu-Tack and watched the small flames as they ate from tins of food.

"How far are we from Hallow Hope?" said Violet, chewing with her mouth open.

"About eight miles. We're close."

"Not close enough to walk there tonight."

"Maybe."

"It'd be stupid to keep walking in the dark."

"I know." He sipped water. Held one hand up to the light, noticing the faint tremor under his skin. "What if we get there and they're gone? I don't know what I'd do."

Violet's eyes were solemn. "Would you give up?"

"I don't know."

"We could try and get off the mainland," she said. "What's it like in the rest of Europe?"

He put the water bottle down. "It's about as fucked as it is here. Wherever you go, it's fucked."

"So, is this it then?"

"What do you mean?"

"The end. The end of us; of the human race."

"Who knows? We don't know how the other parts of the world are doing, but the last we heard, it had all fallen. Parts of the United States could be surviving. Canada and South America. The Middle East is probably the same old shit storm. No idea about China or Russia. I think it's the same all over the planet, to be honest. The Plague Gods have won."

"I've always wondered how North Korea would have coped."

"Who knows? Who wants to know? I don't want to know."

"Maybe there's a survivors' colony in Greenland or Alaska; or the Antarctic."

"Maybe," Morse said. "It's not impossible."

"What about the tribes in the Amazon?"

"Fuck knows." He rubbed his aching face.

"It's insane," said Violet. Her eyes were watery in the candlelight. "One day everything is rosy – fast food, iPhones, Starbucks, Google – everything at your fingertips. And now it's all gone."

"Extinction level event. A lot of it was overrated anyway. We'd fucked things up even before the plague arrived."

"Do you know what I miss most?" she said.

"What?"

"Custard donuts."

"I miss chips with brown sauce."

"Nice one."

Morse smiled at her, and she smiled back, but the moment soon died when she had to wipe her eyes and turn away.

# CHAPTER FIFTY-FOUR

The infected attacked during the night. It started with scraping at the walls and then the front door was hammered upon by a scrum of bodies all clamouring to get inside.

Morse and Violet stood together in the hallway and faced the demented groans and vile shrieks from beyond the house.

"We have to fight," Violet said. She sounded terrified.

Morse wriggled his fingers around the shaft of the crowbar and nodded.

"Get ready."

The front door didn't hold for long until it was splintered and ripped down. And then the infected came inside with their black claws, thrashing limbs and choking mouths. Glimpses of wet tendrils writhing in the dark.

Morse attacked the first infected through the door – a shivering abomination of a naked man – and it fell back with its face crumpled inwards. Violet used her lump hammer to crack a woman's skull open.

The next infected creature rushed forward with sharp fingernails and gnashing teeth. Violet hit the creature around the side of the head and pushed the knife into its stomach.

The infected came towards them, scratching at the walls and floor. Morse swung the crowbar double-handed and knocked a teenage girl off her feet; she hit the wall before she lunged forward again, and he brought the crowbar down and collapsed the top of her skull. She lay writhing at Morse's feet until he stamped on her throat, crushing her windpipe and snapping her neck.

More infected poured through the doorway. Morse and Violet exchanged a glance.

"Good luck," she said.

Morse nodded at her. "Ready?"

"No, but fuck it."

"Good."

They screamed and rushed towards the infected, weapons held high, murder in their hearts. And all about them was flesh and blood.

\*

In the first light of the day they stood exhausted in the mist outside the house, with the corpses of infected all around them, some still twitching or wheezing their last breaths. Everything stank of the plague and the insidious pestilence.

Morse dropped the bloodied crowbar, his arms trembling, and put his hands on his thighs as he hunched over and vomited onto the ground. His clothes were covered in gore and his face was speckled with blood. His heart hurt. When he'd finished expelling the contents of his stomach he stood and looked at Violet as she crouched by the broken body of a little girl. She was crying. He walked over and stood beside her.

Violet didn't look up at him. "She looks like my niece."

The girl's scalp still retained a few wisps of blonde hair. Her bloodshot eyes open and lifeless. The dress she'd been wearing on the day of her infection was little more than strips of filthy rags over her emaciated body. It had been a blue dress. Prominent ribs. Her hands were more like claws. Her stomach was perforated with stab wounds.

"It's not her," Morse said.

"I know." Violet tossed her knife away and it clattered on the road. The blade thick with drying blood. "But when I saw her, I thought it was Julia, and I hesitated and she almost had me because of it. I never knew what happened to Julia. I last saw her with my sister, running towards a refugee shelter as a swarm of infected poured down the street. There was no way they could have escaped."

Morse touched her shoulder.

"They were all people, Morse. They all had ambitions and hopes and fears and worries. They loved and hated and they had dreams, and now it's all nothing. And I had to end it for so many of them."

"Come on," Morse said. "Let's get cleaned up."

She let out a deep sob and wiped her eyes. "Okay."

# CHAPTER FIFTY-FIVE

They left the motorway and took the A39 later that morning. Five miles from Hallow Hope. There was thunder in the east, crackling and roaring, and it sent a shiver through Morse's bones. The thought of facing a Plague God turned his heart to cinders and drained the strength from his legs. What would he have to confront to save Florence?

"There's something ahead," Violet said as she slowed her pace. "Looks big."

Morse saw it rise from the mist and thought it was some species of infected monster before he noticed the windows and the curve of a wheel.

They stopped behind the back end of a minibus. Morse looked further into the mist where it revealed the convoy of vehicles. Morse moved forward and Violet followed. Minibuses, vans and Land Rovers.

It was all abandoned, deserted. No bodies. The backs of the vehicles were loaded with belongings, baggage and supplies. Cold engines.

"Where have they gone?" Violet toed a dropped handkerchief. "Why would they leave all their stuff behind? Why would they leave the vehicles with fuel still inside?"

Morse stood watching the vehicles. "Let's walk down the road and find out."

*

A mile later they found the bodies half-eaten and dismembered. Ripped flesh and skin upon the blood-red road. Throats slashed. Hanging tongues. Vacant eyes.

This was the Order of the Pestilence, or what remained of it.

Morse looked down at the cadavers scattered across the road, searching for Florence's corpse among the remains, but the sheer violence of their deaths made it impossible to identify anyone. His eyes were hot and stinging, and he felt sick. The smell was of slaughterhouses and carrion rooms.

"I can't see Florence anywhere." His voice was weak and unsure. His legs felt unsteady. The ground seemed so far away. A mounting pressure reared inside him as he tried to hold the trembling of his hands while stepping over severed body parts, hair and peeled skin. Offal-stink made him dizzy.

"It was a fucking slaughter," Violet said. "It's like they just disembarked willingly from the convoy and came here to be killed. Like cattle."

"It doesn't make sense," Morse said.

Violet stood next to him and put her hand on his arm. "I don't think Florence is here. We'll find her."

Morse had never before noticed the blueness of her eyes.

"It's okay," she said.

He nodded and wiped his mouth.

She smiled at him, with something like hope.

He touched her arm. "Thank you."

The bullet made a neat hole in Violet's forehead before the back of her head was blown out. Her eyes met his, and she opened her mouth to say something, before her legs failed and she collapsed at his feet.

He stared down at her, shocked into silence, her blood warm on his face and hands. His mouth hung open as he tried to say her name, but all that spilled out was a trembling breath.

The next bullet took Morse in the shoulder.

# CHAPTER FIFTY-SIX

His hands scraping raw on the tarmac, Morse crawled over the road as someone came through the mist after him. The shoulder of his coat was soaked with blood. He gritted his teeth at the pain and dragged himself to the roadside and sat against the wheel of a rusted car. His body had failed him and this was the end. Faint and sick, he clasped one hand to his shoulder to stem the bleeding, and all he could do was look at Violet's body lying on the road.

A shape manifested in the mist and struggled towards him, hunched upon a walking stick.

"You bastard," Morse said.

Jardine emerged and stood looking down at him with such an expression of hate and anger that Morse almost turned away. The old man looked at the pistol in his hand. The weapon he'd used to kill Violet.

"You didn't have to kill her," Morse said, and spat at him. "You motherfucker, you didn't have to. What was the point? Why? You fucking bastard…" His voice faded with his strength.

"Hello, Morse," Jardine said.

"Pointless death, all of it." Morse gritted his teeth against the agony in his shoulder and stared at the murderer.

Jardine wiped his mouth. "She had to die. It seems that we all have to die. Are you ready to die now, Morse?"

"What happened to your army? Looks like the infected fucked up your plans."

Jardine winced as he touched the weeping wound in his side. His face clammy and bloodless. "I was betrayed."

"Betrayed?"

"We were slaughtered. The infected were waiting for us. The Plague Gods were in the sky. When we first arrived, it was exciting and I thought we were going to be welcomed. But after we all disembarked from our vehicles and walked for about a mile, the infected emerged from the mist and set upon us. It was a massacre."

"What about Florence? Is she dead?"

Jardine's eyes fluttered. He grimaced. "They didn't harm the children."

"Then how did *you* survive?"

"I managed to escape while the others were slaughtered. I hid. I heard them all die, Morse. I heard the infected feeding. And when I returned, the infected were gone and they had taken the children with them, down the road to Hallow Hope."

"Ascension," said Morse.

Jardine's face crumpled as if he was about to cry. "I was supposed to be their leader, but only the children were saved. Why wasn't I saved? I have the gift. Why didn't they take me with them?"

Morse shook his head. "Maybe you weren't pure enough. Too old. Too weak. Just a doddering old man."

"Don't you mock me," Jardine spat. "Don't you *dare* mock me, you insignificant wretch."

Morse savoured the taste of blood in his mouth and raised his middle finger to the old man.

Jardine shook with rage and his eyes were wild. He took one step forward, breathing through his clenched jaw. "I should have killed you back at Darlington House. I should have cut your head off."

Morse mouthed *fuck you*.

"Bastard!" Jardine bared his teeth and aimed the pistol at Morse's face.

A plaintive cry drifted out of the mist.

Morse saw something monstrous approach behind Jardine and he thought it was the Devil arriving to take them both away. He grinned through nerve-shredding pain and felt a pure wave of relief for the first time in a long while.

"Judgement," Morse whispered.

"What?" Jardine said, puzzled.

"You'll see."

A tall form of flailing tendrils came out of the mist behind Jardine, seized the sides of his head with dripping pincers and lifted him from the ground. He screamed and dropped the pistol. The monster emerged fully, and the sight of it almost stopped Morse's heart. It was over ten feet tall and pale white in colour, shuddering on insectile legs that bent both ways at their joints. The squirming appendages on its glistening abdomen danced in the air, whip-like and tipped with weeping stingers.

And those stingers jabbed at Jardine's body, piercing him multiple times through his clothes. His face slackened and blood frothed from his mouth as he gurgled and spluttered. More pincers emerged from flesh sheaths within the creature's centre mass and gripped Jardine's limbs; and his final scream died as he was torn in half like a wet cardboard effigy and his insides slopped upon the road and steamed in small mounds.

The creature opened its vertical maw and pushed the two parts of Jardine inside, gobbled up his dangling legs, and then there were only the sounds of bones being snapped and flesh chewed to paste.

Morse's chest tightened. A squeezing hand around his heart. He stared in awe at the monster, waiting for it to come forward and work itself upon his quivering body. He felt his mind slipping away, and it was for the best, because he did not want to be aware when it fell upon him.

The monster skittered forward until it towered over him. Its smell was of stagnant water and brine. Jardine's blood stained its mouth and limbs. A shivering breath slipped from its maw. Morse saw the teeth inside gnashing in anticipation of his flesh.

"Hurry up and get it done," he said. "I've had enough. We've all had enough."

The monster's appendages descended to him and paused before his face, wriggling and floundering, dripping a pale fluid onto his clothes. One of the appendages touched his forehead and he had to stifle a horrified cry by gritting his teeth. The appendage's sharp tip ran across the skin of his brow but didn't break the skin. He swallowed bile down his throat. The back of his mouth watered with nausea.

"What are you waiting for…?" he whispered.

The monster backed away until it was indistinct in the mist, and it stayed there watching him, a tumultuous form mewling softly, sated by the feast of Jardine's body.

# THE LAST SOLDIER

Another form melted from the mist and approached, stepping softly over the corpses. A small, slight figure that smiled and reached towards him. A girl he once knew. He tried to stand, but his legs failed and his ailing heart was a terrible weight.

The girl stood and looked down at him. Her scalp was completely hairless and her eyes were soaked in a deep red. The gown she wore hung from her thin shoulders, speckled with dried blood. Her mouth was pretty, and when she smiled again Morse felt the pain leave his body. He smiled back at her. His dark angel.

"Florence," he whispered.

She reached down for him and took his hand and her skin was warm. "You came back for me. I'm sorry I was mean to you before. I'm so glad you're here."

"What's going on, Florence?"

She showed her teeth. "Something wonderful has happened, Morse. It's all going to be okay. There will be no more pain. No more death. Not for any of us"

"What do you mean?"

"Come with me and I'll show you."

# CHAPTER FIFTY-SEVEN

The Plague Gods filled the air while Morse and Florence walked hand in hand to the cries of monsters in the mist. The air he breathed was foul with rot and thick enough to be swallowed like fluid. Shapes moved around them, barely glimpsed. Nasal snorts and murmuring. Deformed faces stretched beyond human suffering. Crooked bodies lurching and loping. Beasts of the plague, misshapen to obscene positions and composed of human limbs, faces, eyes and torsos. A prehensile tail tipped with a loaded stinger, weaved through the mist. A bloated stomach glistening as it peeled open to allow a sheathed proboscis to emerge wetly, draped with strands of mucus. The slapping of flesh on the ground. Feral cries.

Florence was smiling. Her voice was serene and kind, as if she'd been dosed with some kind of opiate. "Don't be scared, Morse. Nothing will hurt you here."

Morse turned his head slightly, trying not to stare at her hairless scalp or meet her red eyes, which looked like deep pools of velvet. He tried to keep the fear out of his voice, despite the tremble of his mouth and chin. His heart was frantic.

"What happened to you?" he said.

Her smile never wavered as she raised her face to him. "I know I seem…different, but I'm still me. I'm still the girl you know. I've just been *changed* a bit, that's all."

"Is this your ascension?"

"This is the prelude to it. I'm in the early stages of transformation."

"What will you become?"

"Something wonderful. It'll be glorious, Morse. The Plague Gods have welcomed us."

"They didn't welcome the Order of the Pestilence."

"They weren't gifted, so they were deemed irrelevant. Only good for food, I'm afraid."

"What about Jardine? He had the same gift as you."

"He was just a facilitator, though an unwitting one. His purpose was to bring the children together, and once he'd fulfilled his purpose he was no longer needed."

Morse realised that the other children were standing nearby, silent and motionless in the mist, watching him and Florence. They were red-eyed and hairless. The boys and girls of the plague. He thought of them as larval forms eager to shed their human skins and reveal the monsters lurking underneath.

"Why haven't you killed me yet, Florence?"

She wiped her mouth with back of her pale arm. "I want you to join us. There is no other way. This is the next stage."

"You want to infect me, you mean."

She halted. "Look ahead at what is waiting for us, Morse."

He stared into the mist as it swirled and capered, and when it thinned and allowed him to see beyond, it revealed an enormous pit whose edges faded into the vapour. The ground had collapsed or been scooped out. Endless. Incomprehensible. Nothing but darkness within. He stepped forward until he was a few yards from its edge and felt such a wave of vertigo that he held his arms out to steady himself.

"That's what's left of Hallow Hope," Florence said. A note of victory in her voice. She'd appeared beside him, gazing down into the abyssal dark.

"What happened here?" Morse said, trying to comprehend what his eyes showed him.

"The Plague Gods came down from the heavens," whispered Florence. She trembled with something like excitement. "This is how it's supposed to be."

"I don't understand."

"You won't be a drone; you'll be something else. Something better. Something greater."

"Like what?"

"A protector. A guardian. *My* guardian, again."

A deep rumble travelled underneath their feet, like massive tremors in the deep earth. Morse swayed and almost fell down, but Florence gripped his hand and held him up. The tremor passed beyond them. Morse didn't let go of her hand despite the damp meat feel of her skin.

"What do you mean?" he said.

She turned away and faced the pit as something emerged with the sound of colliding mountains.

"Oh god."

"Yes, that's right," Florence said. "A god."

The immense form rose and extended into the sky, at least four hundred feet tall. A gargantuan entity that roared through a mouth as wide as a quarry, claiming the world and all life upon it. A wavering, writhing protean form, extending giant tentacles towards the sky, casting the ground in shadow, its red skin rippling and swelling with undulating tendrils and immense worm-like appendages.

Morse retreated from the pit until he fell onto his back, staring up at the monstrous titan. The Plague God. One of many. He felt his mind slipping away. His heart jerking in his chest. Hard to breathe. He realised he was crying and biting into his fist so hard that his teeth left dimpled marks in his skin. He couldn't speak.

Florence stood over him as he put his hands to his face and stared through the gaps between his fingers.

Past her, membranous-winged beasts swooped, circling the towering Plague God, screeching and wailing. They were pale, elusive forms, darting around the massive tentacles like birds or bats. His eyes hurt, and he tried to deny what he saw, but there would be no denying of anything because this was the way of things now. This was the plague in all its forms.

Florence offered her hand and he accepted. He could feel her alien heart beating. The corruption within her spreading like cancer. "This is the fate of all sentient life," she said. "The other children and I will be emissaries to other worlds yet to receive the plague."

"Emissaries?"

"The plague has evolved, Morse, and it wants other life forms to accept infection willingly. Communion is so much easier that way."

She pulled him to his feet and he stood there breathing weakly, grasping his shoulder. He glanced beyond her at the abomination that filled the sky; the Plague God in all its dark glory. Florence unhanded him but stepped closer until he could smell her. The foul odour of her mouth and her bloodless skin.

"I can talk to the Plague Gods. All the children can. We're linked. Our thoughts are shared. The Plague Gods have agreed to let me take you, Morse. We can still be together."

He reeled, pleading to her with his eyes. "I can't join you like this, Florence. This isn't life. This is wrong. It's not supposed to be like this."

Doubt passed over her face. "There is no other way, Morse. Human survivors are slowly being wiped out or absorbed, and soon there will be no one left. Come with me, Morse. I can save you from an agonising, lingering death. What will you do if you flee? You'll die out in the wastelands, or become infected and you'll join the swarm and you'll just be another drone. This is the only way. Come with me, Morse. Please."

She held out her hand.

Morse swayed on his feet, wiping his eyes. "I don't know. I need time to think about this. It's all too much." His heart winced. He put one hand to his chest.

"Take my hand," she said. "It's the only way."

He met her crimson eyes. She was still the girl he'd sworn to protect, but she was being consumed from within and it broke his heart beyond comprehension.

The children gathered around them. No one spoke. The thunder roared in the sky. Writhing flesh in the mist all about them. The sky darkened with colossal shapes.

He sagged, torn by indecision, the sounds of the Plague Gods filling his skull. He looked at Florence. Saw her the way she had once been. The little girl he'd rescued from an abandoned refugee camp. The girl he'd saved. The girl he'd come to love as a daughter. And then he saw the truth of her: transformed by the Plague Gods, changing into something that would soon be unrecognisable as human. She would be lost.

She was already lost.

His mouth trembled and he let out a low, mournful moan.

Florence reached for him. Her small voice. "Come with me, Morse. We can be together until the universe dies."

He let out a low sob.

She touched his arm gently, like old times.

With one hand he reached behind him into the waistline of his trousers under the hem of his coat and grabbed the pistol stashed there. The pistol that Jardine dropped when he'd been plucked from the ground and devoured. And Morse pulled the pistol free and brought it forward and aimed at Florence. His hand was shaking terribly, his shoulder in agony. Screeching laughter filled his head. He was losing his mind. He muttered with no idea of the words he spoke.

The children wailed around him, except for Florence; she simply watched him with her red wine eyes full of sorrow and disappointment. They became watery with what seemed to be tears. And she knew what would come.

Morse grimaced at the pain of the bullet wound and wished to die soon. "I can't let you become a monster, Florence. I love you. You are my daughter. My girl. My weakness. I promised to protect you, to save you, and I will. I will save you from the monsters."

Florence opened her mouth and shrieked his name as he fired the pistol into her chest. The report of the gunshot filled the space between them, and the silence that followed was terrible and heart breaking. Morse cried with such sorrow that he fell to his knees.

The children stumbled away, clasping hands to their faces and vanished into the mist.

Morse closed his eyes for a moment and exhaled deeply until there was no air in his lungs. When he opened his eyes, Florence was lying on the ground, sprawled cruciform. A red rose spreading upon her gown.

He sobbed. "I'm sorry. I'm sorry." He knelt next to Florence and held her hand, lowering his face next to hers. "I had to save you."

Her mouth took weakening mouthfuls of air. She looked at him with tears in her eyes, and she became that frightened little girl he'd saved once upon a time.

"Forgive me, Florence. Forgive me, please."

She raised her head slightly and whispered something in his ear, but it was too soft to be heard and she died with her mouth close to his face as a final shuddering breath rattled in her chest.

He cradled her head and kissed her brow. She was already cold. He cried for a long time, surrounded by the hell of Hallow Hope, as the Plague Gods roared and screamed and mourned for his loss.

"I love you, Florence. Sleep well, my girl. It's all over."

# EPILOGUE

The world was darkening and the skies were never without thunder and rain. Black fungi bloomed and flourished and expelled spores that killed the trees. Plant life withered and died. All creatures of the plague prospered in the ravaged land. Swarms of infected merged to form monstrous, writhing titans of flesh. This was the next stage. Their evolution, witnessed a thousand times on a thousand different worlds.

A new ecosystem was emerging. New monsters and beasts. Abominations and obscene things that lived to kill and feed. Terrible infants born from monsters' eggs. Broken gods birthed from nightmare wombs. The world was flesh, tooth, maw, stinger, and claw. It was meat and skin. A world torn asunder to be remade.

The fate of all life.

Joseph Morse had fled Hallow Hope with Florence in his arms. He staggered for miles, on the verge of collapsing, until he found a place in a drenched field and laid her down on the ground and held her hand and said he was sorry for failing her.

He tried to dig a grave with his bare hands, but the ground tore his nails and scraped the skin from his fingers. He cried and shouted to the sky. He wailed for the lost world and the countless dead. Florence, Violet, Tomas, Karen, Sophie. There was nothing to be done.

He covered Florence with broken branches and dead leaves and then stood on tottering legs and said goodbye. He put the pistol to his head and squeezed the trigger, but there were no bullets left for him. And all he wanted was one. A small favour. But even that was beyond him now.

Morse dropped the pistol into the mud and looked down at Florence's shrouded form. His last goodbye. His last apology. Then he walked away into the mist, whispering old prayers to dead gods.

\*

He was a long time upon the southwards road, and when he arrived at the town, dying and wheezing, shuffling in torn trainers and cowering in the rain, he fell to his knees and started laughing. And it was good to laugh because there was nothing else to do. He hadn't drunk water or eaten in days and his body was already consuming itself.

This was the town where he'd grown up. The place he'd left when he'd joined the army. This was the first time he'd returned since then. Almost thirty years ago.

# THE LAST SOLDIER

He walked the lifeless streets and his childhood haunts. The shadows of his youth. Those days of changing from a boy to a young man. All of it despondent and abandoned, mouldering, fading to rust and silent sorrow. The old fish and chip shop. The greasy spoon he sheltered within when he was hungover and hungry. Shops vacated and emptied long before the outbreak. The houses of old friends. The bus shelter where he'd had his first kiss and a quick fumble with the neighbour's daughter. He couldn't remember her name. The recreation field where he used to play football with his mates. The lanes and alleyways he'd cycled down. The pubs he'd frequented in his late teens, and those he'd been thrown out of for fighting. Street corners and fast food. Drunken memories. Young women in short skirts.

All of it gone now. And his recollection of those times was waning as his heart dwindled in its beating, ticking down to the end.

The world was now the domain of the Plague Gods. They walked the earth and ruled the sky. The planet was being adapted to suit them. He thought the air was getting thinner, but he wasn't sure if it was merely the failing of his lungs. Not that it mattered, because he had no plans to see the next morning.

After stumbling along the streets for an hour he finally arrived at the road where his parents lived. He stood in the street and turned in a circle and observed the houses in their straight rows. They all seemed intact, although they were slowly falling into disrepair. He walked down the road and stopped outside his parents' house. The front door was closed. None of the windows were broken. Unscathed from the horror of the last two-and-some years.

His father's car was still in the driveway.

His heart quickened. Almost thirty years. Christ. He shivered, coughing into his hand, blinking at the rain.

He opened the gate and stepped onto the pathway between the overgrown sections of lawn. An old bicycle against the wall. A bird table. A spade. The front door was locked. He bent down and retrieved the key from under a large painted pebble. For some reason he couldn't explain, he had known it would be there.

Turning the key and opening the door he stepped inside into the hallway, flanked on one side by coats on hooks set upon wooden racks. Two umbrellas. A bobble hat and scarf. Shoes lined in pairs against the wall. A smell he recognised in the air. Old things. Dust and age.

He entered the living room and found the skeletal remains of his parents together on the sofa. Standing there, staring at their huddled bones, he spoke to them and apologised for the crime of being a bad son. He asked for their forgiveness.

Around him on the shelves and the mantelpiece were photos of him as a boy or teenager. Polaroid images he could only look at for a short while before tears filled his eyes. A photo of him as a curly haired tyke, throwing a stick for their old dog to chase. Another one featured him and his dad on Lyme Regis beach, making a sandcastle; the sun must have been behind his mum when she took the photo, because her shadow was painted on the sand next to them.

Morse slumped in an armchair, weighed down by regret and sorrow, sick with shame and the dreadful knowledge that he had the chance to make peace with his parents but not the courage to do so. He put his head in his hands and stayed that way for a long while, until he raised his face towards his parents and let the tears well in his eyes. They had died together and that was some comfort to him. But they had died without knowing what became of their son, and that was something that couldn't be forgiven, not even by the kindest of saints.

*

He struggled up the stairs, gripping the banister tight with both feeble hands. On the landing he hunched over and clasped at his chest until the pain abated. He opened a door with his name upon it and crossed the threshold, swept away by memories as he stood on the threadbare carpet.

His parents had never redecorated his old room. The walls were plastered with faded posters of Eighties' football stars and glamour models. An ancient hi-fi lurked in one corner, covered in dust, next to a portable black-and-white television. His *Commando* comic books stacked upon a shelf, next to the football annuals he received as Christmas presents each year. Old VHS tapes of war films. His Airfix Spitfires and Hurricanes. Copies of *The Eagle*. His Tottenham Hotspur duvet cover. The companies of die-cast soldiers arranged in their ranks.

The floor still creaked in the same places.

He closed his eyes and remembered his mother shouting up the stairs to tell him his dinner was ready or to rouse him from bed on school mornings. He recalled the time he'd brought Stacey Jarvis back here when his parents went out one night. The things they had done in his bed. Their frantic attempts to dress after his parents returned early from the pub. His dad's laughter when he found them.

He smiled to himself, but it was tired and pointless, and he had to sit down on the bed to rest his legs. His bones hurt and the wound in his shoulder throbbed with infection. He could feel his inner workings slowly shutting down, and bowed his head as his heart slowed and spluttered like a broken engine. Not long to go. And he was relieved and grateful to die as a man. To die human. It was a rare gift in these final days.

He pulled back the sheets and climbed into his old bed, and he lay there saying the names of all the people he'd known over the years. He apologised to anyone he'd hurt or cheated or let down, and when all that was done and he could remember no more, he closed his eyes in the comfort of the place he called home and listened to his heartbeat gently fail while he imagined the happy times of childhood.

# THE END

# ABERRATIONS of REALITY

"Obsessively dark and razorous, these graphic takes on life, faith, illusion and self-delusion open paths where you need to watch your step." —Tanith Lee

## Aaron J. French

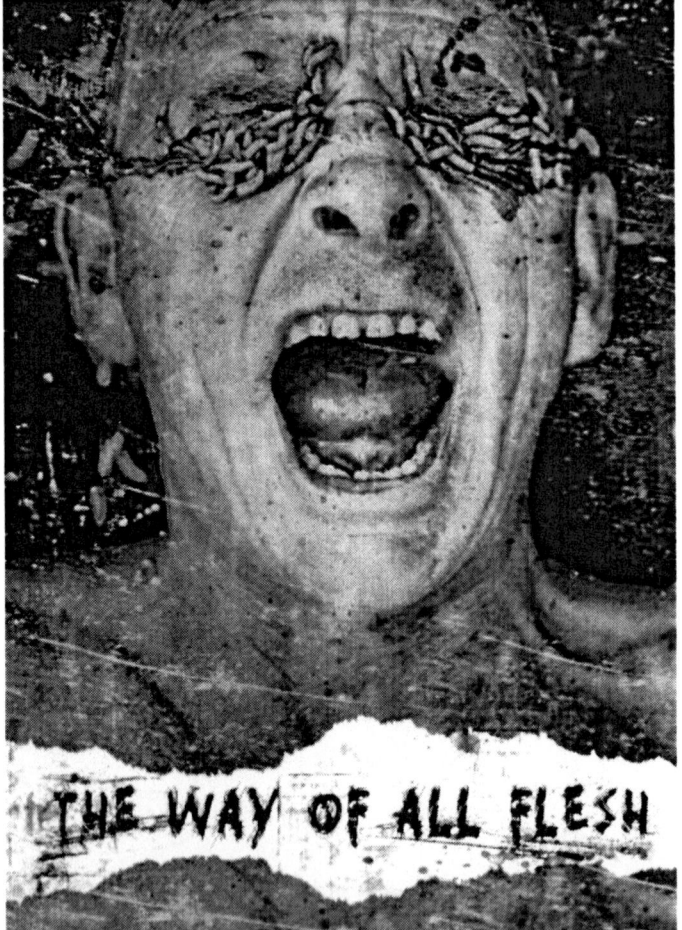

# Of Devils & Deviants

## An Anthology of Erotic Horror

GRAHAM MASTERTON
TAYLOR GRANT
MAYNARD SIMS
RALPH ROBERT MOORE
CLAUDE LALUMIÈRE
AARON J. FRENCH
ADAM HOWE
JOHN McILVEEN
C.W. LaSART
LUCY TAYLOR
JEFF GARDINER
CHRISTIAN A. LARSEN
SHAUN MEEKS
MANDY DeGEIT
CAMERON TROST
J. DANIEL STONE
KENZIE MATHEWS
ERIC LaROCCA
STACEY TURNER
JENN LORING
KENNETH W. CAIN
KEN MacGREGOR
BEAR WEITER

INTRODUCED BY BRAM STOKER AWARD-WINNING
AUTHOR, LUCY TAYLOR

COMPILED AND EDITED BY
ADAM MILLARD & ZOE-RAY MILLARD

Lightning Source UK Ltd.
Milton Keynes UK
UKOW02f1055250516

274963UK00004B/108/P